HARLEQUIN®

Western Romance

THE BULL RIDER'S PLAN

Jeannie Watt

HARLEQUIN

Western Romance

Romance—the Western way!

AVAILABLE THIS MONTH

#1665 A TEXAS SOLDIER'S CHRISTMAS
Texas Legacies: The Lockharts
Cathy Gillen Thacker

#1666 THE COWBOY SEAL'S CHRISTMAS BABY
Cowboy SEALs
Laura Marie Altom

#1667 A SNOWBOUND COWBOY CHRISTMAS
Saddle Ridge, Montana
Amanda Renee

#1668 THE BULL RIDER'S PLAN
Montana Bull Riders
Jeannie Watt

ISBN-13: 978-0-373-75784-8

EAN

"Take me with you." The words came out before the thought was formed.

The look on Jess's face was priceless. It also ticked Emma off. "I'm not kidding."

"You can't come with me."

"Why?"

"For all the reasons I've given over the years when you wanted to come along with me and Len."

"I'm not underage anymore." She was twenty-five, but he probably didn't realize that. He started to speak, but she interrupted. "I can drive part-time, which will come in handy if you get yourself all beat up, which is a very real possibility." He opened his mouth again, and again she jumped in. "I have a little money socked away. Not enough to start a new life, as I'd hoped, but enough to buy food for myself for four weeks."

Jess eyed her, obviously waiting for her to run out of steam before telling her no way.

"You can buy the gas, because you'd be doing that no matter what."

Jess waited a few more seconds, then said, "Are you done." It was a statement rather than a question.

Dear Reader,

I knew five sets of identical twins growing up. I went to prom with an identical twin. Several years later, my husband and I were watching a television show about identical twins who married identical twins at the twin gathering in Twinsville, Ohio. I was able to point at the screen and say, "The one on the left was my prom date." I could tell them apart even then. Funny thing, once you get to know identical twins, they don't look so much alike.

I truly enjoyed writing my twins stories—*The Bull Rider's Plan* and *A Bull Rider to Depend On*. Jess and Tyler Hayward look alike, but they have opposite personalities—like many of the identical twins I know—so I was able to craft two very different stories. Tyler was a wild child who depended on his brother to bail him out of trouble, and Jess is the responsible twin who needs to loosen up and follow his dream. Writing Jess's story was particularly fun because I gave him a heroine, Emma, guaranteed to drive him crazy. Jess needed some crazy in his life, although in the beginning he would not have agreed with me.

I hope you enjoy reading Jess's story. Please feel free to stop by my website, jeanniewatt.com, to learn more about me and my books or to sign up for my newsletter. I'd love to hear from you!

Happy reading!

Jeannie

THE BULL RIDER'S PLAN

Jeannie Watt

HARLEQUIN® WESTERN ROMANCE

Recycling programs
for this product may
not exist in your area.

ISBN-13: 978-0-373-75784-8

The Bull Rider's Plan

Copyright © 2017 by Jeannie Steinman

Printed in U.S.A.

Jeannie Watt lives in southwest Montana on a small cattle ranch and hay farm. Before moving to Montana, she spent many years living off the grid in Nevada ranch country and teaching at a rural school. When she's not writing, Jeannie enjoys running, sewing, reading and having electricity available at the flip of a switch.

Books by Jeannie Watt

Harlequin Western Romance

Montana Bull Riders

The Bull Rider Meets His Match
The Bull Rider's Homecoming
A Bull Rider to Depend On

Harlequin Superromance

The Brodys of Lightning Creek

To Tempt a Cowgirl
To Kiss a Cowgirl
To Court a Cowgirl
Molly's Mr. Wrong
Wrangling the Rancher

The Montana Way

Once a Champion
Cowgirl in High Heels
All for a Cowboy

Visit the Author Profile page at Harlequin.com for more titles.

To Jake, the best calf rider in the family.

Chapter One

There were times when a guy needed to be alone with his thoughts.

This wasn't one of them.

Loud voices and louder music washed over Jess Hayward as he pulled open the rear door of the Shamrock Pub and stepped inside out of the light June rain. After too many nights spent alone, second-guessing himself, he wanted noise and lots of it. A way to shut off his brain and focus on things other than the fact that he'd just given up a steady job to follow the rodeo for four weeks.

It was the right choice. His twin brother was tearing up the professional bull-rider circuit, and Jess knew he should take a shot before it was too late. He was a good bull rider, better than Tyler in some respects, but he was also cautious—not about rough stock, but he did have a backup plan for when things went awry. That was why he was going the rodeo route. If things worked out, he'd join his brother on the pro circuit come January. If not, he'd go back to work for the construction company that sent him all over Montana overseeing the assembly of steel-framed buildings.

But even though he'd made his decision, it was

surprisingly hard to shut off the voice of sanity and reason—possibly because for most of his life he'd been that voice for both himself and his brother. Tyler had a penchant for wild behavior—or he had until he hooked up with his now-wife, Skye Larkin. Jess was no saint, but compared to Ty, he was…well…kind of boring.

No. Not boring. Careful.

He crossed the crowded floor to where his friend Gus Hawkins was standing behind the bar. He waited his turn behind a group of college girls, smiling at one of them when she turned and gave him a flirtatious once-over. Apparently, she liked what she saw.

"Hi," she said with a dimpled smile. "I'm Talia."

"Jess."

Talia's friend turned and pushed a drink into her hand, then made a gesture toward a group of guys on the other side of the room. Talia gave a helpless shrug as her friend grabbed her wrist and started pulling her away.

"Maybe I'll see you later," she called with a laugh before disappearing into the crowd.

Maybe. It'd been a while since he'd dated anyone and he felt kind of rusty. Something about twelve-hour days and being on the road too much. Well, he was about to be on the road too much again, but in a different way.

"This is a surprise," Gus said as Jess stepped forward to rest his hands on the edge of the bar. "For a minute, I thought you were Tyler."

"Easy mistake to make." Even their mom made it sometimes.

"Because even though he's on the road most of the time, I still see more of him than I do of you."

"And that will continue," Jess said. "I'm hitting the rodeo circuit."

Gus gave a satisfied grunt. "Finally."

"It's now or never. The body's not getting any younger." Taking a beating on a bull was truly an occupation for the young.

Gus set a glass in front of him and poured a shot. "On me. For luck. How are you traveling?"

"Bedroll in the back of my truck."

Gus held up a finger before moving away to take an order from an old guy in a cowboy hat. He drifted back toward Jess and said, "Take my camper. I'm not using it. I'm just too lazy to sell the thing online."

"That would be…great." It would certainly beat the bedroll in the back of the truck, which was how he and his brother had operated during the three years on the Montana circuit before Tyler went pro and their parents sold the family ranch and moved to Texas. At that point, Jess realized that neither he nor Tyler would have a place to live if one of them didn't get a full-time job and keep the home fires burning. Tyler hadn't really needed home fires, because he was rarely at home. When he finally did come home for a spell, he'd moved onto a neighboring ranch and had become engaged to the owner.

That had been a turning point. That had been when Jess decided that maybe he did have enough money in the bank. That he was only responsible for himself, which was an odd feeling for an identical twin.

"When are you leaving?"

"Tomorrow afternoon for Union City."

"Come by and see the camper tomorrow morning. If it'll work, take it."

"I'll pay you—"

Gus leveled a deadly look at him. "I don't think you will."

Jess simply nodded. He'd pay something if he used the camper, but he'd wait until he got back rather than argue with Gus now. He continued to stand at the bar, talking to Gus as he drank. Across the room, Talia smiled at him and raised her glass in a small salute. He smiled back, thinking it might be time to make his move. But before he could push off the bar, a small crash at the other end made his head jerk around.

Emma Sullivan's wide gray gaze came up from the mess of broken glass and beer on the bar. She instantly started apologizing to Gus's uncle Thad, who was standing only a few feet away.

"I'm so sorry. That guy bumped into me." She began stacking the smaller pieces of glass onto the larger pieces as she attempted to clear the mess.

"No harm done—or there won't be if you stop trying to pick up the glass," Thad said sternly.

"Sorry." Emma pulled her hands to her chest, holding her fists against the blue-gray sweater she wore. Her eyes came up again and this time she zeroed straight in on Jess. Her lips parted as she recognized him, then she looked over her shoulder at the door.

Excellent. Unless he was misreading the signs, Emma, his late best friend's little sister, had had too much to drink.

He set down his whiskey. "I'll be back," he said to Gus. Just as soon as he made certain that Emma wasn't alone.

"Jess," she said as he approached. She attempted to sound offhand, but the end of his name came out just slurred enough to confirm his suspicions.

"Are you here with someone?" he asked, reaching out to take her elbow as someone jostled her from behind, making him think that her story about the guy bumping her was true.

"Watch it," he growled. The guy turned, half ready to defend himself until he saw the deadly look in Jess's eyes. He gave a grunt and moved a few feet away. Jess turned back to Emma. "Are you here alone?"

"I came with Jonesy, but I haven't seen her in a while. I think she might have left with someone." She spoke the last part in a stage whisper that had Jess rolling his eyes.

A table close to them emptied and he gestured toward it. "Sit. I have to get my drink."

Drawing in a breath, he headed to the other end of the bar, retrieved his whiskey, which he might as well enjoy, because it might be his last drink of the evening, and headed back to where Emma sat with her elbows on the table.

"What's going on, Em?"

"My drink spilled when that guy bumped me." She gave him an encouraging look. "I could use another."

"I'm not buying you a drink." He refrained from saying she'd had too many, because nothing brought out the fight in Em like being told she couldn't do something. Or that she had to do something. Something about being one of the youngest members of a large blended family. Her stepmom had her hands full raising a lot of kids, but that didn't keep her from trying to control every move they made.

She tightened one corner of her mouth, which was wide and full and frosted with shimmery stuff. He used to tease her about her mouth being too big for her face, but he'd been wrong. She'd finally grown into that smart mouth of hers. It looked…good. And the corners were once again drooping.

"Selma is driving me crazy," she suddenly blurted, as if needing to explain why she was in the Shamrock alone, having a few. "I need to get married to get her off my back."

Jess downed the rest of his whiskey and considered ordering another. Across the room he saw Talia flirting with another guy, then turned his attention back to Em. "Are you thinking about getting back with Darion?"

"No." The word came out flatly. Adamantly. Her broken engagement would stay broken. "But that's not slowing Selma down. If she doesn't quit hounding me, I'm going to—" she moved her hands back and forth in a gesture of frustration "—*do* something."

"Wait a minute. *She* wants you to patch things up with Darion?" Which wasn't the same as Darion wanting to patch things up.

Em leaned closer and he was suddenly aware of the crisp floral scent that was so her. He remembered how she smelled because she spent so much time hanging around him and Len, driving them crazy when they were younger, wanting to be part of whatever they did because Len was her "real" brother. Her full brother. And now he was gone.

"She wants me to wear the freaking dress that she paid too much for." She lowered her voice for another stage whisper. "As if I asked for it. For the record, I did not. I wanted the five-hundred-dollar dress, but she liked the other one." Emma leaned closer still and her long reddish-brown hair brushed over his arm like a whisper of silk. "She wants to impress the neighbors.

Outdo Marilee's wedding. Since I'm the only girl in the family, I'm the only shot she has."

"Come on, Em. She isn't going to encourage you to get married just so she can pour money down a wedding rathole."

"Oh, yeah?" She sank into her chair. "Well, she can't get her deposits back. The money is already poured."

Jess gave his head a shake. "Not much anyone can do about that."

Emma's expression brightened. "Maybe you can take Darion's place? Just for a while? Fake wedding? Keep Selma happy?"

"I'd rather take a bullet in the leg."

Emma's mouth drooped again. "I had a feeling you'd say something like that."

"Nothing personal, Em."

"Yeah." She leaned back in her chair and started surveying the room, as if trying to pick out another husband prospect.

"Do you want a ride home?"

A look of horror crossed her face. "No." She cleared her throat, trying to sound nonchalant as she said, "I'm no longer staying at home."

"Then where?"

"Starlight."

"The motel?"

"Howard lets me park my truck in his garage."

Howard had been one of Em's friends in high school, but probably wasn't on her mother's radar because he was kind of shy and retiring. "Mom knows I'm okay because she stops to see me at work, but I won't tell her where I'm staying. I'm one step away from blocking her number, too." She gave a small snort as she stared down at the table. "I'm surprised she hasn't tailed me."

Jess knew from growing up with Len just how intense Selma could get when she was on a mission.

"How do you know she hasn't?"

"I watch my rearview mirror."

"Things were that bad with Darion?" Bad enough to call off a wedding? Although he had to give her credit for calling it off six months before the big day instead of waiting for the last moment.

She let out a breath. "I don't want to talk about it. Besides, I refuse to marry him just to get Selma to leave me alone."

"But you'd fake marry me."

Emma smiled. "Because it's you. There'd be no complications."

"Ain't going to happen." Besides, he wasn't certain if *anything* went down with Emma without complications. Even getting engaged to one of the nicest guys he'd ever met hadn't kept things from getting complicated. No one knew exactly what happened with Em and Darion, and it didn't appear that Jess would be the exception to the rule. One minute they were on, the next the wedding was off. Darion was now working up north in Kalispell, having left right after the engagement was broken, and it didn't appear that he was coming back anytime soon.

"How are you getting home tonight? To the Starlight, I mean."

Her shoulders sank a little. "Good question. It looks like Willa did leave with someone." Just as Jess had hoped to do. Well, that wouldn't be happening. Talia had her arm linked with a tall cowboy who seemed satisfied with the way his night was playing out.

"I'm going that way."

"You barely got here."

"I think it's time to leave. I'm taking off tomorrow, so maybe a decent night's sleep is in order."

"Yes," Emma said in a mock stern voice as she got to her feet. "One must get their eight hours a night. And eat three square meals a day. And brush their teeth two—"

Jess took hold of her arm and gently propelled her forward. "What do I owe you?" he asked Gus, who waved his hand.

"See you tomorrow morning. Bring back some big purses."

"That's the plan," Jess said. He glanced down at Emma, who looked as if the booze was hitting her harder now that she was standing. "Do you have everything?"

"Everything except for a husband."

"You're not getting one of those here." He put an arm around her, drawing her close to his side to keep her on her feet as they negotiated the crowd. Again, her light floral scent drifted to his nostrils, and Jess was surprised at how well he remembered it. Well, it was said that traumatic memories are often triggered by scents, and while his experiences with Emma didn't qualify as traumatic, they did qualify as annoying.

When they stepped out into the damp evening air, Emma gave a small shiver. Jess's instinct was to pull her even closer, but instead he eased back, putting a hand on each shoulder and steering her toward his truck. She was keeping her feet well, but he wasn't taking chances.

"So you're into purses?" she asked as she negotiated around a puddle.

"Rodeo purses."

"I have one of those. Lots of silver and fringe—"

"Prize money, Emma."

She clapped a hand over her mouth, then dropped it and said, "I wasn't thinking rodeo because, well, you haven't been competing much. That's embarrassing."

"For a girl who used to chase cans, I imagine it is."

Emma had been one hell of a barrel racer, because the word *caution* never appeared in her vocabulary. She'd stopped after Len had been killed in the rollover accident on the road leading to their ranch.

He felt her stiffen and figured her thoughts were following the same line as his. He opened the door and handed her up into the truck, thinking that he'd probably never touched Emma this much, ever.

She let out a breath and let her head fall sideways against the window when Jess got into the driver's seat. He headed for the Starlight—an older, yet immaculately kept motel on the edge of town—and slowed to pull into the lot when Emma jerked suddenly. An instant later she was practically on the floor.

"Drive on."

"What?"

"Don't. Pull. In." When he looked over at her, she was scrunched down so far that she was invisible from the outside. He scanned the parking lot, then saw what had Emma curling up into a ball. Her younger brother Wylie was parked at the far end of the lot. And if he wasn't mistaken, there was another Sullivan ranch truck parked next to him. Selma, no doubt.

"Take me to your place," Emma murmured.

Jess opened his mouth to say "No," but the utter desperation in her voice made him shut it again. He abruptly put the truck into gear.

"Thank you." She spoke so low he barely heard her.

"I think you can sit up now."

She pushed herself upright and let her head fall back again, squeezing her eyes shut. "I don't feel so well."

Jess stepped on the gas. Ten minutes later they were at the field that he called home. After his twin moved out, Jess had never felt cramped in the small camp trailer he lived in while saving money. He was going to feel cramped tonight.

After parking near the trailer, he started around to the passenger side of the truck. That was when he realized—too late, of course—that he'd parked too close to the big puddle that had formed during yesterday's long rain.

"Em—"

Down she went. He heard her scramble and curse, and by the time he got around the hood of the truck, she was getting back to her feet and wiping wet hands down the sides of her pants.

"This sucks."

"Sorry."

She frowned at him first and then at the puddle next to her, all but invisible in the darkness, since he hadn't bothered to leave the porch light on.

"Where are we?"

"My place."

She looked around the dark field where his trailer, the only man-made structure within a mile, was parked. "Are you sure?"

"Positive. Come on." He took hold of her elbow as

they walked together toward the trailer, but Emma pulled free.

"I could have used you a few minutes ago. I'm fine now."

"Whatever," he muttered. He unlocked the door and opened it, then stepped back as Emma climbed the metal steps. He followed her into the trailer and snapped on the light before closing the door, thus trapping the two of them in too small of a place.

You can't abandon Len's little sister.

The truth was that he wouldn't have abandoned her even if she wasn't related to Len. That wasn't the kind of guy he was. He'd watch out for Emma until she was in a proper condition to do battle with Selma, who wanted her to wear the dress.

How stupid was that?

Emma grimaced down at her wet jeans, then shook her head as if thrusting the matter out of her mind.

"What's all that stuff?" she asked, pointing at the canvas duffels and plastic storage containers.

"That's my life for the next month."

"The rodeo. Right." She lost interest and swayed just a little as she crossed the tiny room and sat on the seat under the window. "Can I sleep here?"

"Sleep in my bed."

"Where will you sleep?"

She seemed only mildly interested in the answer as she once again slumped sideways.

"Tyler's bunk." The small built-in bed in the hallway leading to the tiny bedroom at the back of the trailer.

"I'm fine here..." Em's voice started to trail off. She was fading fast. Jess crossed the room and pulled her up to her feet, ignoring her muttered protests.

"You'll do better in the bedroom." That way he could get up, make coffee, start his day, while she slept it off. He propelled her down the hall, opening the door just before his bedroom. "Bathroom," he said. He opened the bedroom door and pointed inside. "Your bed." He turned her so that she was square with the bathroom. "Are you good?"

"The best," she muttered before taking a stumbling step into the bathroom and closing the door in his face.

Jess shut his eyes, let out a breath.

Len would want him to do this.

Chapter Two

Emma woke with a start, pushed herself up on one elbow, then collapsed with a low groan as her brain let out a mighty protest.

Where was she?

Think.

She tried. Her brain was still playing games with her. She opened her eyes again, took in the clues. She was in a rumpled bed in a travel trailer—

A surge of relief washed over her. Jess. She was with Jess Hayward. She was safe from her mom. Safe from her mother's friends.

But for how long?

It wasn't like they could march her to the altar and make her marry Darion, who would have a few things to say on the matter if it came to that. But they could make her very, very miserable. Darion had cut and run after they'd canceled the wedding, and was currently hiding out in Kalispell, but Em didn't have that option. She had a job at the local café. She had no qualms about quitting, but she also had only a small nest egg to support her if she moved elsewhere—which left her at the mercy of Selma, the control freak.

There was a loud thump from the other end of the trailer and a muttered curse.

Jess, who'd given up his bed for her.

Well, he owed her for the crappy way he'd treated her in the past.

Em pushed back the covers and sat on the edge of the bed, waiting for her head to clear. Dear heavens, but she'd kill for orange juice.

Maybe Jess had orange juice.

She reached for her pants, which were in a heap on the floor, grimacing as she realized they were soaking wet. A memory started to crystallize…tripping, hitting the puddle next to the truck, going down…

Embarrassing.

She shook out the pants. There was no way she was pulling those clammy things up her legs, so she got out of bed and opened the closet. There, on a shelf, was a stack of neatly folded jeans. She'd been hoping for sweats, but jeans would do. Sitting back on the bed, she pulled on the Wranglers. Jess was lean, but the pants still hung low on her hips. She bent down to roll the cuffs and instantly wished she hadn't as her head started pounding harder. Aspirin was also a necessity.

She looked around the bedroom for her purse and came up empty. Hoping against hope that she hadn't left it at the Shamrock, she put on the sweater she'd worn the night before and then quietly opened the bedroom door and slipped into the bathroom.

Yes. Ibuprofen. An economy-sized bottle, such as one would expect to find in the medicine chest of a bull rider. Pain was part of the game. Her brother had ridden broncs and she knew about hurting. Em popped two pills, washed them down, then grimaced as she faced her reflection.

She put a hand up to her bed head and tried to push her long unruly hair into a less bent shape. After a couple of pats and pushes she gave up and pulled open the door. It wasn't as if Jess hadn't seen her at her worst.

Although…last night may have been her worst. She was a drinking lightweight. She blamed Jess and Len, who never let her go out with them. She'd never even been drunk until she hit twenty—only one year shy of legal age. As long as her brother and his friend were around, she was well managed.

Now, Jess's twin, Tyler…he was fun. But he was also a friend of Len's and made sure she didn't get into trouble. Life after high school hadn't been as much fun as it could have been.

The curse of being the only girl in a family of boys— although until her father had married Selma, she'd only been the youngest of two. After Len had died, she had only half brothers. Three of them. All younger and all firmly under Selma's thumb. She'd encouraged them to rebel by setting an example, but they remained firmly managed—something she refused to be.

She headed toward the kitchen, a journey of about eight feet, past the bare bunk that Jess must have slept in to the main part of the camp trailer, wondering why she felt so stupidly self-conscious. This was Jess, after all. Worst-case scenario, he'd treat her like she was still fifteen. Best case… She wasn't certain that there was a best case.

Jess stood at the counter staring down at the toaster. He was ridiculously good-looking. Dark-haired with sculpted cheekbones and striking eyes. Her friends had all been mystified as to why she wasn't all over him. She assured them that it was because she knew him. It was his attitude. As in, he had this attitude toward her. So…she'd had an attitude toward him.

Yet here they were.

He suddenly looked up, meeting her gaze. Oh, yeah. Those were some eyes. Her memory wasn't faulty.

"Morning," he said.

"Morning," she echoed, wishing her voice wasn't so thick.

His eyes strayed down to her legs. "Are you wearing my jeans?"

"Maybe?" She automatically hitched up one side as she answered. "You weren't using them." She indicated the duffels with a jerk of her chin. "And it looks like you're packed for your rodeo trip, which leads me to believe you weren't taking them."

"Maybe I wanted something clean to wear when I got home. Besides, that's not the point, Em."

She leaned her elbows on the counter next to him. "What is the point, Jess?"

"The point is that you took my stuff without asking."

"And if I had wandered out in my underwear to ask permission…?" She gave him a how-would-that-have-gone-over look.

"You could have called from the bedroom."

"Oh, Jeh-ess…can I wear your pa-ants?" She raised her eyebrows in a mock innocent expression. "Like that?"

"Yeah. Like that."

This felt like old times, when Jess would go all follow-the-rules on her whenever she came up with a great idea, like going out to party with him and her brother, even though she was underage, and she would argue with him.

"You want me to take them off?"

"No." The word came out so rapidly that it was almost embarrassing. His loss.

"Then I guess I get to wear your jeans." She looked around the trailer. "You have a clothes dryer here?"

"Yeah. Right."

"They make those apartment-size things."

"I go to the Laundromat."

"Pity. Now I have to wear your jeans."

He didn't answer, making her think that he was simply making noise about the jeans. The toast popped and he set it on a plate, then put the plate on the table. Emma took the hint and sat down, even though she wasn't the least bit hungry.

"We're going to talk."

"We are?"

"I brought you to my home rather than leaving you to the mercies of your mom. I want some answers."

She narrowed her eyes, ignoring the fact that it made her head hurt. "What kind of answers?"

He set a cup of coffee on the table next to the toast and then leaned back against the counter, folding his arms over his chest. His expression was don't-mess-with-me serious when he said, "Tell me what's going on."

"You want to know my business?"

"Yeah. I do."

Em studied the table, debating. Other than Darion, no one knew the whole truth. She figured by this time, the conjecture was worse than what had actually happened, and far be it from her to disappoint the local gossips. She looked up at him. He had his stern brother look on. Somehow it didn't seem as effective without Len there to back him up.

"Fine. What do you want to know?"

"Why are you really hiding from Selma?"

Emma planted her elbows on the table and pressed her fingertips to her forehead. Jess knew her family. Knew the dynamics. If he didn't, he wouldn't have done the good-guy thing and taken her to his place instead of dropping her off at the motel where Selma would have had a fine old time making a scene. Em owed him.

"She wants me to marry Darion. She assumes Darion feels the same way."

"He doesn't?"

"No. We broke up by mutual agreement."

"Tell her that." Em leveled a look at him and he cleared his throat. "Right."

"She honestly believes that if she strong-arms us into matrimony it'll all work out. She thinks I have the jitters."

"But you don't."

She gave her head a slow shake, because a fast one would have hurt. He looked like he wanted more information, but she'd gotten as personal as she was going to get. "She won't let it rest. I thought moving into the motel would make my point."

"How much are you paying to stay there?"

"Nothing. I helped Howie get through all his math classes from kindergarten on. He's kind of indebted to me."

"His folks know?"

"I think they think *we* should get married—Howie

and I, I mean." She let her head fall back, closing her eyes. "I need to escape."

"Running doesn't work."

She opened her eyes. "How do you know? Have you ever run from anything?"

"Is this working for you?"

"I haven't run far enough. I can't afford to run far enough."

"Is there such a thing as far enough when Selma is involved?"

"Maybe not." She let out a breath and then took a small nibble on the edge of the toast. Her stomach told her to stop, and she did, setting the toast back on the plate. As to the coffee…she swallowed hard. She truly was a drinking lightweight. "Do you have orange juice?"

"No. I'm taking off later today, so I emptied the fridge. That's why there's no butter on your toast." One corner of his mouth tightened. "You know…if you needed a place to stay, you could stay here."

Emma stared at him. Selma would find her…but maybe not for a couple of days.

And surely she'd give up when Emma started paying her back for the wedding dress she hadn't wanted, which had been a special order and couldn't be returned.

"You know…I think Selma was trying to make sure I didn't back out of the ceremony by buying me that dress."

"What?"

Jess never had been that good at following her thought processes…but neither had anyone else. Her mind did tend to jump around. Even Len had problems and he was the person closest to her. She smiled at Jess—maybe her first smile in days. "I appreciate the offer."

"I'll be gone for the better part of the summer."

"Hitting the circuit?" She remembered the rodeo purse.

"Hitting it hard. I have to decide whether to go pro this January. Time is running out for me."

"I see." She studied the table in front of her, wondering what her next move would be now that Selma had ferreted her out at the Starlight and had brought Wylie along for backup. She'd eventually find her here. Her life would be hell for the next few weeks. Darion would be no help, because Selma thought he also had cold feet and would be as hard on him as she was on Emma if he was foolish enough to come back to Gavin.

Neither of them had the jitters—they had each chosen the wrong person and were doing something about it before it was too late. Selma didn't see it that way, which made Emma wonder about her marriage to her father.

Had they settled? If so, they seemed happy, which only gave Selma ammunition.

If only Darion had cheated on her...or done something outrageous. Then maybe Selma would back off.

"Em...?"

She raised her gaze, met the eyes of the man that she trusted most in this world—even if he did piss her off most of the time. He was the closest thing she had to her brother and right now she needed her brother.

"Take me with you." The words came out before the thought was formed.

The look on his face was priceless. It also ticked her off. "I'm not kidding."

"You can't come with me."

"Why?"

"For all the reasons I've given over the years when you wanted to come along with me and Len."

"I'm not underage anymore." She was twenty-five, but he probably didn't realize that. He started to speak, but she interrupted. "I can drive part-time, which will come in handy if you get yourself all beat up, which is a very real possibility." He opened his mouth again, and again she jumped in. "I have a little money socked away. Not enough to start a new life, as I'd hoped, but enough to buy food for myself for four weeks."

Jess eyed her, obviously waiting for her to run out of steam before telling her no way.

"*You* can buy the gas, because you'd be doing that no matter what."

Jess waited a few more seconds, then said, "Are you done." It was a statement rather than a question.

"Waiting to hear all the reasons that this is a no-go," she said mildly. "Although, you know that Len would have taken me."

"How do I know that?"

Her tone became low and serious. "Because this isn't a matter of me being capricious. This is something I need to do. Selma is breaking me, Jess. I don't want to run forever…just until I can get my equilibrium back."

He was wavering. He, who took the hard line whenever she'd come up with some scheme to include herself in his and Len's adventures.

"I lost my brother a little over a year ago, Jess." Nineteen months, actually. "I'm not one hundred percent. And I think Len's death is affecting Selma, too. I just… want to get away."

He lowered his eyes. Tapped his fingers on the table

a couple of times. Em held her breath. Waited. "What about your job?"

"There's a stack of applications in the office. Skye will understand." Jess's sister-in-law was now managing the café where she worked. She was a friend. "Don't make me beg."

He met her gaze with a frown. "You are begging."

"Don't make me beg super hard, then."

Jess scrubbed his hands over his face, and Emma let out a silent sigh of relief. She'd won. She was going to get her reprieve. "Only if Skye will hold your job for you."

"What?"

"You have to make a living when you come back."

"That's not your concern."

"But it's my condition…that and a rodeo-by-rodeo assessment. If this isn't working, then the deal is done."

Emma wished her head wasn't hurting so much. Yes, that seemed fair enough…except for the rodeo-by-rodeo thing. She did have a way of triggering Jess.

Well, she'd just have to figure out a way not to do that.

JESS THOUGHT BACK over his rides at Hennessey's practice pens the day before. He hadn't hit his head, so he couldn't blame anything but himself for agreeing to let Emma ride along with him on his rodeo tour.

The change in her expression when she'd realized he was about to say yes had been profound and drove home the point that Emma, who had the ability to bounce back from any and all situations, was not bouncing back from the death of her brother and her broken engagement. Throw in a controlling stepmom and...well, he'd said yes.

He hoped he didn't regret it.

Of course you're going to regret it.

Okay—he hoped he wasn't going to regret it too much.

"I need to go to the motel and get my stuff."

"Do you have enough to travel?"

"I'd better, because I'm not going back to the ranch to pick up more."

"But you will tell them you're leaving."

"The beauty of texting."

"And talk to Skye."

"I'll do that today before we leave."

"Are you leaving her in a lurch?"

"No. It just occurred to me that Chelsea wanted to ease back into part-time now that she's had the baby, so this will work out well." She shrugged. "It's almost like it's meant to be."

He didn't know about that, but he was certain that now that he'd said yes, there was no way he could say no—at least not until they started wrangling with one another while on the road.

"I'm driving to Union City tonight."

She gave him a small smile. "We can pick my stuff up on the way out of town."

Chapter Three

Jess didn't have a lot to say when he drove, so Emma read on her phone and left him in peace. Len had always wanted to get into his head before an event, and she figured Jess was the same. And even though she was being the perfect cab-mate, riding in silence, Jess kept cutting looks her way as if expecting her to speak.

What was she supposed to say? *Thank you for taking me with you?* She'd already said that, and Em wasn't a big believer in repeating herself.

On the fifteenth or sixteenth look she finally broke.

"Nice day for a drive."

He frowned at her.

"You wanted me to talk, right?"

"I was wondering why you weren't talking."

"There's nothing to say."

He gave her an I'm-not-falling-for-that look. Fine. He didn't have to fall for anything. She went back to her phone. He wasn't going to be able to complain that she was distracting him from mentally preparing for his ride.

"When did you become so quiet?"

"When I figured out that listening was as valuable as talking." She scrolled to the next page.

"When did that happen?"

She gave a small shrug. "Years ago."

"Not that many years ago."

She couldn't help scowling at him. "I was in college." She'd dropped out shortly after Len died.

"Ah."

That shut him up. Good. She wanted to read… except now she couldn't focus. She turned off her phone, set it in the door compartment next to her. Union City wasn't that far away and once they got there, they'd set up camp. Jess had a camper on the back of his truck that he'd borrowed from Gus. Since Em was short, and grateful to be along for the ride, she'd volunteered to sleep in the truck, thus giving him privacy.

They pulled into the Union City rodeo grounds a little after seven. Jess leveled the camper while Em rolled out her sleeping bag in the rear seat of the truck. Once the bag was in place she walked back to the camper and knocked on the frame of the open door. Jess was already testing out the stove. They'd agreed to take turns cooking on the road and tonight it was his turn.

In Emma's mind, he was lucky to have her along. He didn't have to partner up with anyone to share the driving and he was assured of a decent meal after competition. If he ended up in the hospital, he had someone there to watch his back. Though, honestly, after losing Len, the idea of anyone being in the hospital kind of froze her up.

Emma shoved the thought aside and stepped up into the cramped confines of the camper. Jess continued fiddling with the cooktop, so she stepped to the opposite side and scooted behind the built-in table, the upholstery on the bench catching her jeans and making it hard to slide properly. She propped her elbows on the table as Jess lit a match to test a burner—something she was certain he'd done before they'd left, because he was that kind of guy. He'd no doubt changed the oil on the truck and had the tires rotated, too.

"A little cozier than your last place."

"The price was right." After the burner caught, he leaned back, turning the knob to adjust the flame from high to low before turning it back off again. "Gus Hawkins used it when he was on the circuit."

"Before he came to his senses and started tending bar?"

He gave her a sour look that made her want to smile, but since she was taking pains to steer them away from their old roles—Jess, the rule guy, versus Emma, the rule breaker—she settled for a mere twitch of the lips. Although she'd noticed on more than one occasion that Jess wasn't so much about him following the rules, as he was about Emma following the rules.

Whatever.

"Since the stove is working, can we make some coffee?"

He sent her a look. "And stay up all night?"

"Coffee doesn't affect me that way."

"Then I'll make *you* some coffee."

"Going to have trouble sleeping?"

"Not if I don't have coffee."

"You don't have to make coffee for me. I can do it."

She started to slide out from behind the table, but he shook his head. "Stay put."

Emma shrugged and scooted back, where she leaned against the upholstered foam cushion behind her. Darion would have stepped back and happily allowed her to make coffee. Darion probably wouldn't have minded being in that tight space with her. Jess, on the other hand, had never liked being too close to her—little sister cooties or something.

She let out a low sigh. Why couldn't things have been...*better*...with Darion?

"You okay?" Jess frowned as he filled the small coffeepot. He must have heard her sigh. Well, there were sighs and then there were *sighs*. This was a sigh of frustration, not a sigh of unhappiness, but she saw no sense in trying to explain that to him.

"I'm fine." She spoke lightly. "Just going over some things in my head." He scooped coffee into the basket, then set the pot on the burner. "What's the schedule tomorrow?" she asked.

"I ride. We leave."

"That's what I thought." So much for making conversation, but as awkward as this felt, it was nine hundred times better than dodging her mother and brothers. Not that her brothers were that much of a problem, but they were being nagged by Selma, too. And things would start to feel less uncomfortable between her and Jess as they put more miles behind them.

She tapped the tips of her fingers together as she tried to remember a time that things *had* been good between them. Couldn't come up with one, which made her wonder why she trusted him so implicitly.

Maybe because he was the one guy she'd never been able to pull one over on?

Or maybe because he was such a Dudley Do-Right, as opposed to his twin, Tyler, who looked for and found trouble on an almost daily basis?

Did it matter?

Silence hung until the coffee started perking and Jess filled a ceramic mug up to the brim.

"Thanks." She wasn't about to ask for cream, but she'd be buying some tomorrow.

He nodded, then seemed to be at a loss as to where to perch himself in the confines of the camper.

"Do you want me to take my coffee to the truck and drink it there?"

"Why?"

"You look uncomfortable."

"I'm not uncomfortable. Just…cramped."

"If I went to the truck—"

He let out a pained breath, which seemed to be his favored way of communicating with her, and then sat down on the short L of the bench around the table so that they were perpendicular to one another. She smiled at him over the top of the coffee cup.

"You make a decent cup of joe."

"Thanks."

She sipped, reminding herself again not to do what came naturally and trigger him. She owed him for this opportunity to escape, and since he'd said they would evaluate the situation rodeo by rodeo, she didn't want to screw things up too early.

"I brought cards," she said. "I assume that strip poker is out, but maybe cribbage?"

"Did you bring a board?"

She cocked an eyebrow at him. Selma was an amazing cribbage player—something to do with her utterly controlling personality, no doubt—and she'd taught all of her children to play and play well. There had been no allowing the kids to win in order to build their confidence in the Sullivan house. Definitely a dog-eat-dog card-playing world that Jess had been introduced to when he'd become Len's friend.

"Stupid question," he muttered.

She reached for her giant Western purse with the silver and the fringe and the bling and pulled out a folding cribbage board made of bird's-eye maple. Jess reached out to run a finger over it.

"Len made it for me."

"I remember." A shadow crossed his features, but Emma pretended not to notice. Grief had been her partner for too long and, while she acknowledged it, she no longer let it take over her life—for the most part, that is. There were always weak moments, but she wasn't going to let this be one of them.

She pulled the cards out of her purse, shuffled once and set the cards between them. Jess cut a deuce, she cut an ace and picked up the deck. "I think we should play for money."

"You don't have any money."

"Exactly. I need some." She picked up her cards, quickly choosing two for her crib. Jess debated, chose his cards, then cut the deck. She turned up a jack and pegged two points. "A dollar a point?"

"No." He played his first card and Emma paired it, pegging two more points. And so it went. They played two games, with Emma continuing to have crazy luck. After pegging her last point and skunking him, she drained the last of her coffee.

"This is good," she said as she gathered the cards and put them back in the box. "You used up all your bad luck tonight, so you'll have a good ride tomorrow."

He didn't look convinced.

Emma reached out to lightly pat his face, as she

would have done with Darion or one of her brothers, only realizing as her palm made contact that this was Jess, not Darion or one of her brothers. Dear heavens. *What* was she doing?

And why was her stomach free-falling at the feel of rough stubble beneath her hand?

This was embarrassing.

She forced a smile and casually dropped her hand before reaching for her coffee cup. It was halfway to her lips before she realized that it was empty.

Did she fake a drink or get a grip?

She chose to get a grip and set down the cup. She'd touched Jess's face. Big deal. He'd been like a brother to her for years.

And that was probably why he was scowling at her so deeply right now.

"Sorry," she said. "I do that to my brothers."

"No worries," he said gruffly, but she'd felt him go still beneath her touch, knew that it had startled him as much as it had startled her. "I need to turn in early tonight."

"Yeah. I know." She slid out from the bench. "I want to catch a shower anyway over at the public facilities." It'd been a while since she'd traveled the circuit, and she'd never traveled it as intensely as Jess planned to travel this one, but she knew the drill. On the nights you weren't celebrating or driving, you got to bed early. A worn-out body wasn't capable of peak performance, and with the schedule Jess had ahead of him, he needed to get all the rest he could while he could.

"What time will it be safe?" He frowned at her instead of asking her what she meant. "At what time can I enter the camper and find you decent?"

"Seven?"

"Seven is good. And if you can have the coffee on, that will be even better."

PLAY FOR MONEY. Right. If he and Emma played for money, she'd have to buy the gas instead of him. She was a good player, but she also had the most ridiculous luck. Nobody pulled the fourth jack on the turn up. But Emma did. Len had been good, but Emma was a natural with numbers. She'd gone to college with the hope of becoming an engineer, but had quit after the funeral, settling at home and choosing to work a variety of part-time jobs.

Jess hadn't really kept up with her, but he'd seen her around town, working in various capacities. Funny how Selma was nuts about her getting married, but hadn't hounded her about finishing her education. Maybe because she knew, as Jess did, that Emma would finish it when she was ready.

He rolled over in the bunk. Maybe Selma had wanted Emma to get married because it would help ground her while she mourned. It was a dumb idea, but Selma was also mourning, and people didn't always think straight during rough times.

A good example was him agreeing to let Emma travel with him.

For a while anyway. He didn't see her lasting for all four weeks of his tour, but if it helped her to get away for a while, then he was game.

The next morning he was up early—well before seven—so when Emma knocked, he'd already showered and the coffee was on. He never ate breakfast on the days that he rode, and he rarely ate lunch, unlike his brother, who was counting protein calories and doing yoga. He settled into his head and waited for his ride, going over it, anticipating every move the animal could make, so that his reaction would be automatic. So far it had worked. He had a decent record, but if there was one certainty in bull riding, it was that there was no certainty.

The same rule kind of applied to Emma.

"You have coffee, right?" She was on the pot in a heartbeat, making Jess glad that he'd left her a cup instead of waiting until she got there to make more. He might have to buy a bigger percolator.

She brought the cup to her lips, her eyes closing as she first inhaled and then drank. "Sweet manna of life."

"I didn't know you were a coffee freak."

She slid into her spot behind the table, resting her elbows on the surface and cupping the mug with both hands. "There's a lot you don't know about me."

"Yeah?"

"Yeah," she said, her full lips tilting up on one side. She really did have an amazing mouth. "Telling me to scram didn't make you privy to my many secrets."

He thought about it and had to agree. He didn't know that much about her. Not the things that she held close anyway.

"What do I need to know?"

Her lips started to twitch in a way he didn't like, as if she'd just heard a great joke but didn't want to let him in on the punch line. "What?"

"That jerk Benny Two Feathers just asked me all snide-like if we were shacking up and I told him we were on our honeymoon. That shut him up."

"Good one, Em." He let out a breath. It didn't matter.

It really didn't. And knowing Benny, he fully understood why she'd done that. The guy was a jerk.

He just hoped word didn't get back to Selma. The last thing he needed was for her to set her sights on him as Emma's future husband.

Chapter Four

"You married Emma Sullivan?"

Jess stopped stretching and turned toward Benny Two Feathers, who was smirking at him, as if being married to Em was a bad thing. "We're not married."

"Maybe you should tell Emma that."

"She was yanking your chain," Jess said tightly, settling his hands at the belt of his fringed chaps. "Possibly because you were out of line."

"Hey. I was just curious."

"Yeah. Well, to satisfy your curiosity, Emma is traveling with me to help with the driving." Benny's smirk became more pronounced and Jess had to work to keep his fingers from tightening on his belt. It didn't matter what Benny thought, even if he did have the biggest mouth around. "Em's brother died not all that long ago and she just called off her wedding. She wanted some time away to get her head together. I offered to let her ride along." Kind of. "She doesn't need you spreading rumors about us on top of everything else."

"I, uh—"

"She's my dead best friend's little sister." Jess took a step closer to Benny. "And you'd better leave her alone."

Benny put his chest up, but he didn't have a lot of fight in his eyes as he said, "I meant no harm."

"Doesn't matter what you meant."

Benny gave a curt nod and took a step back. "I'll, uh, tell her I'm sorry next time I see her."

"She'd probably appreciate that."

Jess went back to his stretching, ignoring Benny as he drifted away. One rumor squelched. And since Benny was a talker, everyone would soon know that Em had called off her wedding and that they weren't married. The latter was the more important of the two.

"You're married?"

Jess looked up to see Lara Wynam standing a few yards behind him, her big sorrel barrel horse standing at her shoulder. "I'm not married."

She shot a frowning look toward the field where the competitors parked, then back at him. "That guy."

"Benny?"

"Yes. He told me you and Emma were on your honeymoon."

"He was messing with you."

She drew in a breath. "I have to admit to being surprised to hear you were married. I've never seen you out with Emma."

"She just called off her *real* wedding. She's traveling with me to get away for a while." Jess wondered how many times he was going to have to retell the story. "The canceled wedding, Len's death…get the picture?"

"Oh. Poor kid."

"Yeah. She's pretty broken up. I needed a driver and this worked out for both of us."

Lara's smile brightened and she pushed her shiny dark hair over her shoulder. "Sorry to have jumped you like that. I was…surprised. And I guess it makes sense, since she's Len's little sister."

He and Lara had dated for a while, and he could see where it would be surprising to hear that he was suddenly married. "If you hear anyone asking about my marriage, would you mind setting them straight?"

"I'd be happy to." She smiled again, the dimple that had once so fascinated him showing beneath the corner of her mouth. "Good luck today."

"You, too, WW."

She cocked an eyebrow at the use of her nickname, then turned and led her horse toward the practice arena. Jess watched the sway of fringe across the back of her shirt as she left. Good-looking woman. Center of her own world. They'd parted friends—or as close to being friends as Lara was capable of.

Enough distraction.

He was stretched out; his rope was prepped. The last section of barrel racers was about to begin and after that the bulls would be loaded.

He paced around the perimeter of the chutes, nodding at his competition, but not talking. He'd never been a talker before a ride. Tyler would launch into a long story, excuse himself for his ride, then come back and finish the tale if the guy was still around to listen. Jess had always been the quiet twin.

The cautious twin.

Until he was in the chute, on board the animal. Then he was all about winning.

The last barrel racer did her thing. The time was announced and then the equipment team drove into the arena to remove the barrels before the tractor gave the ground one last go-over. The chutes banged and clanged as the crew loaded the bulls. He'd drawn Lil Bill, which could be good or bad, depending on how Bill felt that day. When Bill bucked, he was dynamite. When he didn't, it stunk because he bucked just enough to keep the rider from getting a re-ride. Jess hoped Lil Bill wasn't having one of his lazy days.

Jess headed to the chute once Bill was loaded, finagled the bull rope into position. Bill stood quietly, which made Jess wonder what kind of ride he was going to have. Bill remained quiet as the bull two chutes down exploded out of the pen when the gate opened, giving Tim LeClair one heck of a ride.

"Watch and learn," Jess muttered to the black-and-white bull when the whistle blew. He eased on top of his mount and double-checked his grip after Chase Wells, a fellow bull rider, pulled his rope tight for him. If this first ride didn't put him in the money, there were other rodeos…but he had every intention of getting to the finals, so he needed this one to be decent. To set the stage, give him momentum.

The gate swung open. Bill set his butt against the back of the chute and refused to move. The gate closed again.

Jess adjusted himself, waited for the gate to open again. When it did, Bill humped up, hesitated, then suddenly reared, blasting out of the chute, exactly as he was supposed to have done the first time.

Despite all signs to the contrary, Bill was in a bucking mood.

When the whistle blew, Jess was close to the fence, where Bill seemed intent on wiping him off now that his job was over. He leaped off the bull, hit the ground, then felt hooves come down on either side of him. He ducked, then as soon as the thundering stopped, dashed for the fence.

Bill made a hook at one of the bullfighters, shook his head at the guy, then with a snort and a flick of his tail, allowed the safety man to guide him to the exit gate.

Jess popped the chin strap of his helmet and headed back across the arena, barely hearing the applause. It'd been a good ride. He didn't know if it would score better than LeClair's, but, in his mind, it should. Lil Bill had gone beyond the call of duty.

EMMA PUSHED OFF from the fence near the chutes where she'd squeezed between two guys to watch Jess's ride. It was impossible to watch a bull ride without feeling a degree of concern, and her heart had been hammering. But now Jess was back on the ground, in one piece, and she could focus on the here and now.

They had a ten-hour drive to the next rodeo tomorrow evening in Brisby, Montana. Emma had no idea if Jess wanted to travel halfway tonight or whether he wanted to leave early the next morning. She'd meant to get a clear answer on that before the ride, but Jess had disappeared before she could ask. Just in case, she'd packed her gear and had it ready to go. It'd be easy to roll her sleeping bag back out on the back seat if he wanted to take off in the morning.

Before she started back to the truck, Jess came out from behind the chutes and stopped to talk to another bull rider, whom she didn't know. It'd been a while since she'd been on the circuit and there were a lot of new faces along with the familiar ones. One face stood out, though, in addition to Benny Two Feathers... Lara

Wynam, whose trailer was parked a few spaces away from Jess's truck.

Winning Wynam.

Emma gave a small snort as she headed back to the truck. Or Whining Wynam. If Lara didn't win, then Lara had an excuse. The arena wasn't properly raked, the gate man sucked, she had her suspicions about the electric timer, yada, yada. Emma didn't bide excuses. There'd been none in her house while she was growing up, and she wasn't putting up with bogus defenses from other people. *Guess what, Lara? Sometimes you don't win. Every now and again, someone might be better.*

Her mouth tightened as she passed the woman's trailer and recalled the fact that Lara always donated heavily to junior rodeo. Okay, she wasn't all bad. Just… privileged. And she complained a lot.

Maybe it was growing up the way Em had, in a blended family with a stern, not necessarily fair, but always controlling, matriarch at the helm that gave her little patience for people who assumed that life was *supposed* to go their way. That wasn't how it worked. She was living proof.

She'd barely reached the truck when Jess showed up, his chaps slung over his shoulder, his bull rope in one hand.

"Didn't win?" The winners were being announced as they spoke.

"Second."

Emma pushed back her hair, holding it against the wind. "LeClair?"

"Yeah." He seemed good with the decision. Emma was not.

"That's bogus. I saw both rides."

Jess's mouth twitched. "The judges saw it differently. By a point."

"At least you're in the money."

"That I am. Ready to leave?"

"I am if you are."

"I thought I'd clean up, if you don't mind grabbing us some burgers for the road."

"Sure."

"And Em?" She shot him a look over her shoulder. "Try to do it without telling anyone we're married, okay?"

She waved her hand at him. "No promises."

The corner of his mouth twitched again and then he started back toward the camper. Emma skirted a few trailers and then had the good fortune to see Benny Two Feathers talking to another rider next to his trailer.

He gave her a look as she went by and half a step later she stopped and reversed course. "Jess and I aren't married."

"I know."

"And we're not shacked up either."

He frowned down at her. "You could have just told me that."

"And you could have kept your creepy questions to yourself."

The guy next to him turned a choked laugh into a cough. Benny gave him a quick narrow-eyed look and the guy simply put his hands up in mock surrender. Benny was a big guy and not that many people messed with him. Emma was one of the few who did.

"I've always treated you with respect, Benny. I expect the same right back." She gave him a nod and continued toward the concession stand, which looked like it was about to close. Behind her she heard Benny mutter a colorful remark that wasn't all that complimentary, but she understood his need to save face. She was good with that, as long as he stayed out of her business in the future.

And hey…she hadn't thought about Selma or Darion in almost an hour.

WHEN JESS GOT back to the truck from the fairground shower facility, which was a whole lot roomier than the facility available in the camper, Emma had a bag of burgers, fries and two giant drinks waiting in the truck. The engine was running and she was behind the wheel. She tilted her aviator sunglasses down as he got into the passenger seat.

"Where are we stopping for the night?"

"Depends on how far you feel like driving."

She gave him a considering look, then put the truck in gear without answering. The field was now close to empty, with only a handful of trucks and trailers remaining. When they reached Brisby the next day, they'd be parking close to a lot of the same people. That was the thing about rodeo—it was like a big traveling family. And like all families, there were members you could depend on and those you avoided.

"So far, so good, wouldn't you say?" Em pulled onto the freeway and eased in behind a truck and Jess made a conscious effort to relax his tense muscles. He'd never ridden with Em before and had no idea whether she was a decent driver or not. As she'd said, so far, so good. She glanced over at him, waiting for a response to her chit-chatty question.

"Would have been better if I'd walked away with

the big money, but all in all not bad." He shifted the leg that Bill had squeezed against the chute. "I could have done without explaining that I wasn't married." Emma only shrugged, again without looking at him. "Spread any more rumors about us before we pulled out?" She gave him a curious sidelong glance and he explained, "Just trying to ascertain what I might be up against next stop."

"No rumors. But I did tell Benny to back off."

So had he. Between the two of them, the guy should have gotten the message.

"Maybe you shouldn't mess with Benny."

"Maybe he shouldn't mess with me."

Jess smiled in spite of himself, then worked his way into a more comfortable position, propping a knee against the dashboard and folding his arms over his middle before closing his eyes. If he could get an hour of sleep, he could take over the driving.

JESS FELL ASLEEP almost instantly, which was something considering the fact that he'd been practically white-knuckled when she'd pulled onto the freeway. To him, she was still Len's little sister, competent enough to help them rope and brand calves, but not ready for prime time in other arenas of life. Fine. It was a role she was comfortable with, the bothersome little sister, and more than that, Jess was comfortable with it.

He was not comfortable with them being pretend-married.

She gave a small snort as she recalled Benny's face when she'd first told him, then glanced over to see if she'd disturbed Jess. He was out, dark eyelashes fanned over the tanned skin above his cheekbones. Her heart bumped a little. He really was good-looking. Maybe it was because she hadn't been around him in well over a year that he seemed different. Or maybe she was looking at him differently. Whatever. She could kind of see what her friends saw—now that he was asleep and not telling her what she couldn't do.

The road straightened out in front of her and traffic was light, so she chanced another glance, curious about why he seemed different. Maybe it was the fact that he'd matured and the angles of his face had become more chiseled, the hollows under his cheekbones more pronounced.

She eased her way around the only car in front of them for miles and then glanced back at Jess. His mouth, which she had to admit was a very fine mouth, was slightly open—and, a split second later, so were his eyes.

Em gave a start as her gaze slammed into his electric one.

"The road." The words were clipped. Not very friendly.

She jerked her attention to the pavement—where'd it'd been one short second before she'd given in to temptation and went for that third look.

"I was just checking on you," she said in a huffy voice.

"To see if I was breathing?"

"To see why you looked different."

He frowned at her. "Different how?"

She kept both hands on the wheel, squeezing it more tightly than she needed to. "I don't know. That was why I was looking."

He sat up straighter.

"You can sleep, you know. It wasn't as if I was staring dreamily at you rather than minding the road. You just happened to catch me midglance."

"Ah."

"And they were fast glances." She demonstrated, exaggerating the speed of her head turns. "Like that."

"Stop."

She smiled a little and relaxed now that they were safely back in their roles, although she couldn't say why the word *safe* had popped into her brain. "I think it's because you've lost weight."

She sensed that he'd gone still and risked his wrath by glancing over at him yet again. He wore a perplexed expression. "I don't recall ever being particularly heavy."

"In your face. You've lost the baby fat."

He muttered something that sounded like a plea to a higher power, then slumped back into his seat. "I don't know if I can sleep if you're looking at me."

"I won't look. Promise."

He let out a breath. Em fought with herself, then glanced over. His eyes were still open.

"That was a trap," she said as she focused on the road.

"That was a test."

"I guess you're going to have to get used to me staring at you when you sleep if you're going to take advantage of having another driver along."

He let out a long breath and closed his eyes once again—Em knew because she looked. "Just...keep it between the lines, okay?"

"I will," she said in a resigned voice. "And maybe, for once, you can have some faith in me."

Chapter Five

Have some faith in her.

When *didn't* he have faith in her?

Like…never.

"Would music bother you?"

Jess kept his eyes closed and readjusted his arms over his chest as he said, "Not if it's low."

"Low it will be."

A second later the last CD he'd been listening to came on and Em turned the volume down. He shifted in his seat yet again and did his best to lose himself in the music and not think about his driver. Impossible. Not when that floral fragrance filled the cab—and not in a bad way. Like Em, it was light and joyful. Em was usually happy—making the best of whatever situation she was in. Scrapping her way through life. True, she'd hit a couple of rough patches recently, but she soldiered on.

So why did she think that he didn't have faith in her?

It wasn't a lack of faith. That wasn't why they, meaning he and Len, hadn't let her pal along with them. It'd been sheer protectiveness.

That and the fact that she'd driven them crazy when she'd been younger, and the perception of the bothersome tagalong sister persisted.

Huh.

He fought the urge to open his eyes and study her, to see how *she'd* changed. Because she had. He'd noticed in the bar that she'd grown into her mouth and, what had once been almost comically oversize in her delicate face, was now perfect—nicely shaped, wide, but not too wide. Full. Kissable.

Kissable?

He shifted in his seat, hoped Em thought it was so that he could get more comfortable. Was *kissable* a word to use in regards to his best friend's sister?

He cracked open an eyelid and thanked heaven that Em was concentrating on the road, as she was supposed to be. Her chin was slightly lifted, her eyes focused straight ahead, giving him an excellent view of her profile, lips and all. Even as he tried to tell himself that a mouth was a mouth and Em's mouth was no more kissable than any other woman's, his body stirred.

Oh, man.

This is Em. Len's sister. Remember that.

So much for sleeping. Jess let out a breath and pushed up into a sitting position.

"Can't sleep?" Em asked, not looking at him.

"Too much adrenaline."

"Huh. I used to totally crash when I was done with a barrel run."

And he usually crashed after a bull ride, if he didn't have to drive several hundred miles to the next rodeo. Adrenaline had never been a problem before—and it wasn't the problem now.

What business did he have thinking salacious thoughts about Em?

Get a grip. You didn't go anywhere near salacious. You just finally noticed that she was a woman, not a kid.

And again he was lying to himself. He'd noticed a long time ago that she was a woman.

She was, however, off-limits. She'd always been off-limits and he'd never allowed himself to think of her in any other way. And now she had issues to deal with and the last thing she needed was the guy she trusted, the guy she was depending on to help her straighten out her life, throwing yet another monkey wrench into the mix.

Jess opened the burger bag. "You didn't eat."

"Not really hungry."

"Yet you bought yourself a burger."

"I'll eat it later."

"When it's cold?"

"Look who's talking. That thing you're about to bite into isn't exactly steaming."

"I don't mind cold burgers. I eat them a lot on the job. I'd buy burgers at night before I headed back to the motel, and pack them for my lunch the next day."

Em wrinkled her nose, but again did not look at him. He found himself wanting her to look at him—just a quick look so that he could assure himself that he was back in control. That he didn't really feel anything but brotherly affection for her. It was Em, for Pete's sake.

"What exactly do you do? I know it has to do with construction, but...what is your job?"

"I travel around the state—well, a lot of states, really—putting up steel-framed buildings."

"*You* put them up?"

"I oversee the crew." And if bull riding didn't work out, he'd try to get his job back.

"Ah. So you were the boss. You should have been good at that."

"Why?"

"Think about it, Jess. You're always trying to boss me around."

Jess smiled a little and felt himself relax as he took another bite of the cold hamburger. As long as Em kept talking, he had nothing to worry about.

EMMA HAD TERRIFIC peripheral vision, and she'd watched Jess watch her when he was supposedly trying to go to sleep. More than watching, he'd been studying her. Like the classic bug under a microscope.

What gave there? Especially after he'd said he didn't want her watching him?

He seemed normal enough now, as he ate cold fries and a cold burger and gave her driving advice, which she really didn't need, but pretended she did, to keep the peace. She had the strong feeling that he was actively looking for things to advise her on—things that she could probably figure out herself, such as the pothole big enough to swallow the truck. *Yes, Jess, I was totally going to drive into that thing and break an axle.*

Things felt a little...off.

Great. Here she was trying to get her life back on track and now she had something else to figure out. Although she hadn't thought about Selma's MPFEL— Master Plan for Emma's Life—since she'd started driving. And the stress that seized her up whenever she did think about it wasn't quite as bone crushing as before. Must be the many miles between them.

As to Darion, well, she didn't mind thinking about

him, because they'd been in deep mutual agreement the last time they'd spoken. Bullet dodged. End of story.

In some ways, she felt closer to Darion now, after they'd done the hard thing and faced up to the fact that their relationship was pleasant, but not much else. Going through life with a friend wouldn't be the worst thing in the world—unless one wanted some excitement in their life. Emma had missed excitement, and trying not to involve herself in things that bothered Darion hadn't been easy for a girl that tended to shoot from the hip. He'd always been a good sport, but…yeah.

"Watch—"

"I see it!" Like she could miss the truck parked on the shoulder of the road with orange cones leading up to it. She eased into the passing lane as soon as the car behind her whizzed past, giving the truck a wide berth.

"Just making sure."

"No. You're micromanaging and I've had enough of that for a while. Okay?" She frowned at him. "And don't complain about me looking at you when you've been doing the same to me."

Amazingly, color started to creep up out of his collar.

Em jerked her gaze back to the road. What the heck?

"The way you were studying me made me wonder if you were plotting revenge for telling Benny we're married." So not true. The way he was studying her made her think that he was trying to figure out something about her. Like maybe why he'd brought her along.

Even if they were still working out the kinks of their road trip, she was not ready to go home and face Selma. And she didn't feel an iota of shame about that. Nothing wrong with hiding out until you were strong enough to deal.

"I'm not a revenge kind of guy."

"Ah. I see." She pretended to have profound interest in his revelation—which wasn't exactly news to her. "I'm not *too* deeply into revenge. But I can't say I don't enjoy a good comeuppance."

"What about Dean Montego?"

Emma shrugged. "Comeuppance." She gave him a bland look. "You *know* what he did to me." Put two live chickens in her car while it was parked at school. It had taken her hours to get rid of all the chicken "residue."

"Totally uncalled for," he agreed. "But you know he was only trying to get your attention."

Emma ignored his last remark.

"If I'd been the revenge sort, I would have reported him to Animal Control." But she'd chosen another tactic. For weeks following the chicken incident, Dean encountered...eggs. Lots and lots of eggs. Eggs in his PE clothes. In his truck. In his locker. She'd even finagled his younger brother into hiding eggs around his bedroom. Finally he'd asked her to stop. So she did.

She drew a breath in through her nose. Dean had never bothered her again. In fact, he'd developed a grudging respect, and when they'd worked together on community activities, he'd been almost friendly.

"Guess Dean didn't know what he was getting into when he engaged you."

"You don't mess with a Sullivan," Emma said on a sniff.

Selma might have been controlling, but she certainly hadn't coddled her kids. The Sullivans had backbone...

although her half brothers could have shown a little more where their mother was concerned, but they were still young.

He smiled at her. "Maybe that's why I'm not plotting revenge?"

"Yeah, yeah, yeah." He wasn't one bit afraid of her.

"You should eat something."

"Fine. Peel me a cold burger."

He laughed and Emma felt an odd pang. She hadn't heard him laugh like that since Len had died. Not that she'd seen him all that often, but when she had, he'd been super serious. Part of it might have been grief. The other part…she didn't know. Jess had always been responsible, but at some point he'd become almost too responsible.

Some people said it was because with wild man Tyler as his twin brother, he looked somber by comparison, but that wasn't it. Jess was in no way somber—or at least he hadn't been when Len was alive.

He peeled back the wrapper of the burger and handed it to her. Their fingers brushed and she found the contact oddly comforting.

"You sure you trust me to drive with one hand?" She cocked an eyebrow at him.

"Yes. I trust you to drive with one hand." The words came out flatly. She'd just bitten into her burger when he added, "You know I haven't ridden with you since Len taught you to drive."

Her chewing slowed and then she swallowed. That was an excellent point. "Okay… I'll give you a pass. However, you do realize that was eleven years ago, right? I've driven a few times since then. I have zero moving violations. I pay lower insurance rates because of my safe driving record. I—"

"All right." Jess lifted his hands in surrender. "I give up."

"Thank you. Now how far do you want me to safely drive you tonight?"

THEY DROVE FOR five hours before pulling into a public rest area that allowed overnight vehicle stays. Jess had fallen asleep after their last stop for gas and woke with a start.

"We haven't wrecked," Emma said drily. "We're at Four Trees."

"I knew that."

"Uh-huh."

Jess let himself out of the truck and stretched out the kinks. He could feel the day's ride, but all in all he felt good. Now, if he could continue feeling good, it would go a long way toward making the finals.

Em got out of the truck and pocketed the keys. "I'm going to hit the facilities, then turn in."

"I'll walk you over."

"Thanks." The lot was well lit and there were three other camp trailers there, but one never knew. Emma opened the door of the women's room, looked in, then gave Jess a thumbs-up. He leaned against the brick wall and waited. When she came out, she gave a small shrug. "There's a shower in there."

"You can use the one in the camp trailer when we get to Brisby tomorrow."

She smiled at him. "I was hoping you'd say that." She looked toward the truck, then back at him. "I can, uh, make it back on my own, unless you want me to stay here to watch your back."

"I think I'll be okay. But if you hear a scuffle…" He grinned at her and she smiled back, then headed across the parking lot to the truck as he ducked into the men's. When he got back, she'd already retrieved her sleeping bag from the camper and was rolling it out on the back seat. All the gear he'd stashed there was now sitting on the front seats.

"We'll take off around six tomorrow," he said.

"That late?"

"Yeah. That late. We'll get there by noon. I ride around four."

"Got it." She jerked her head toward the truck. "I'm turning in."

He nodded and started for the camper, feeling shifty about Em sleeping in the truck while he slept in relative comfort.

A deal's a deal. She said she didn't mind sleeping in the truck. It was the only place she could sleep, short of sharing the bunk with him or converting the bench into the second bed. And then they'd be sharing a very small space. A space without a lot of privacy.

It was best if they continued with the deal they'd agreed upon.

He only hoped that she didn't lose the only set of truck keys he had.

Chapter Six

Brisby, Montana, was a sleepy town under normal circumstances. The big Fourth of July celebration wasn't
normal circumstances. Even though it was July 2, the
town was practically bursting at the seams. The rodeo
ran Friday, Saturday and Sunday, as did the rodeos in
Red Lodge and Livingston.

Jess had drawn decent bulls in all three, so the master plan was to ride in Brisby on Friday, drive the four
hours to Red Lodge on Saturday, and then two hours
to Livingston on Sunday. After that they had a whop-
ping two days off before they headed north to the Coyote Creek Roundup.

After parking the camper, Em took off to explore the
town, leaving Jess to prepare for his ride. She promised
to be back to watch, but when the grand entry began,
he'd yet to see her. Not that it mattered. She was probably up in the crowded stands.

As the rodeo progressed, Jess scanned the crowds
until finally he saw her, sitting near the top, aviator sunglasses perched on her nose, her reddish hair looking
even redder against her green shirt.

And even though it shouldn't have mattered, he felt

better after spotting her. Because he wanted her to watch him ride? Or because he knew where she was?

Either way, she was there. He was the last guy up, which he didn't mind one bit, since he knew exactly what score he was aiming at. The win or loss would be a done deal when they announced his score.

The stock was exceptional at the small rodeo, and only two guys had ridden successfully when Jess climbed on board Paw Paw. Eight seconds later, after what felt like eight minutes of body-pounding bucking, spinning, twisting and rearing, he dismounted, landed on his feet and punched the air. Two successful rides.

When the winners were announced, he was on top. By two points.

He'd won the day. On Sunday, he'd have word if he'd won the event, since there were no finals at Brisby. Winning the day was good enough, because he had a feeling that he was going to win the whole thing. He checked out the stands, but the place where Em had sat was now empty. Fine. He'd catch up with her at the truck and decide what they'd do that evening, since they weren't pulling out until the next morning.

"Jess!"

He turned to see Chase, who'd once again pulled the bull rope for him as he prepped for his ride, and Dermott Kane, a bull rider from the Dillon area, approaching.

"Looked good," Chase said.

"Felt good," Jess replied. "You guys up tomorrow?"

"He is," Dermott said. "I had surgery on my elbow. Have to sit out a couple more." He jerked his chin toward town. "We're going out tonight, us and a few others. Some barrel racers are coming, too." His eyebrows went up as he mentioned the women. "Meeting at the Short Branch on Main in about an hour. Want to join us?"

"Sure. I'll check with Em to see if she wants to go."

"Em?" The guys exchanged a look that told Jess that while they may not have heard the marriage rumor, they were curious as to who Em was.

"Emma Sullivan. She's my driver." *That's all. Nothing more.*

"Oh, yeah," Chase said. "Red hair. Chased cans. Haven't seen her in a while."

"She stopped barrel racing when her brother died."

"Yeah. That sucked."

No argument there. Jess told Chase and Dermott that he'd see them in an hour or two, then made his way back to the truck, nodding his thanks when people congratulated him on taking the day. Em was sitting in the front seat of the truck, knitting. The door was open and her phone was playing music.

"Congrats," she said as he approached.

"Did you see the ride?"

"You beat LeClair by *two* points."

"Should have been three," Jess said straight-faced. "My bull bucked harder."

"You think?" She shaded her eyes at him.

He shifted his weight as her meaning sunk in. "Are you saying that LeClair should have won?"

She considered for a moment, her needles once again clacking away. "All in all, he might have had the better ride."

"No."

She gave him a mild look. "You asked. I answered.

In my opinion, you should have won Union City and he should have won today."

Jess let out a breath. "Whatever."

"It was still a great ride."

"Thanks." He sucked in a breath. "I'm heading out with Chase and Dermott tonight. The Short Branch. Want to come? Warm hamburgers. Cold drinks?"

She shook her head. "I think I'll stay here. Eat at the concession. Have an early night."

"You're sure?"

She lifted her eyebrows. "Totally."

He gave her a frowning look, but she was once again focused on her knitting, counting stitches under her breath. Okay, then.

He started toward the camper feeling ridiculously deflated. She was off base about his score. He'd dominated today…and besides, hers was only one opinion. Only the judges' opinion mattered. And they'd agreed that he'd won. By two points.

EM FINISHED THE row and then set her knitting aside to watch the people as they milled around the grounds. Even though the rodeo was over, there was still a crowd because of the carnival and the outdoor craft and gear show. She'd gone through all the booths before the event, and had bought yarn and needles at a lovely booth that featured knitting supplies, quilting material, soaps and candles. The purchase had set her back, but she figured that by skipping a few meals, she'd be okay, and it was wonderful to have something to do with her hands during her downtime. Knitting had always calmed her, but she hadn't picked up needles in a long time, having been more focused on escaping Selma than in calming herself. Now, she had midnight blue yarn and a lot of it. Enough to keep her busy knitting scarfs and hats for Christmas presents over the next several weeks. Fortunately, everyone in her family looked good in blue.

She'd sent a text to Wylie that morning, telling him that she was doing well. She might need space, but she didn't want her family worried about her. If she was gone long enough, maybe one of her brothers would do something to distract Selma, and then maybe she could slip back to Gavin, start living life again.

Maybe she should sign one or more of her brothers up on an online dating site…

She snorted softly and stuffed her needles and yarn into the plastic yarn bag. Selma wouldn't rest until all her children were settled—no matter how crazy it made them.

"Sure you don't want to go?" Jess had appeared out of nowhere while she'd been lost in thought. She glanced over to where he stood beside the open door, his dark hair damp from what must have been the quickest of showers. Of course, in the tiny camper, a long hot shower was hardly an option.

And he smelled good.

Really good.

"Last chance."

Something stirred inside of her as he stepped closer to the open door, making it a whole lot easier to say, "No. I'm good here. I'll have an early night."

A wild shriek went up as one of the carnival rides fifty yards away began to spin. Jess cocked an eyebrow at her. "I don't think so."

Em met his gaze, saw the challenge there and set the yarn bag on the seat. "Fine. I'll go."

He gave a satisfied nod and stepped back so that she could get out of the rig. "We're walking, right?"

"I don't think we could park any closer to the bar than this."

The town was packed.

"I'll grab my coat." She slid out of the truck and walked past him to the camper where she got her denim jacket out of her bag. Jess followed and locked the door after her.

"If I come home earlier than you, I may need the key."

"If you come home early, I'm coming with you."

She frowned at him as they started across the grass to the street leading to town. "Am I your excuse to get to bed early?"

"Maybe." He gave her a look that told her the real answer was no. He would leave with her because that was the kind of guy he was. Women didn't walk home alone on his watch.

And that was fine, because Emma wasn't a fan of lonely streets during wild rodeo events.

They walked in silence for almost a block before Jess felt the need to break it. There was an odd vibe between them, as if something needed to be addressed— some matter that they were both avoiding…except there was no matter, and he wasn't avoiding anything. And Emma? She might be avoiding Selma, but in general, the girl hit life head-on. Not the avoidant kind. But the feeling persisted.

"I didn't know you knitted."

She pushed her hands into her pockets. "I started in high school, after Len moved out. I like the monotony."

"You like monotony?" He didn't think so.

He heard her let out a small breath and glanced over at her. Her gaze was down, focused on the cracked asphalt. Her hair swung forward over her shoulders, looking redder than usual under the streetlights, and he felt like reaching out and tucking the strands behind her ear so that he could see her face better.

"Maybe that's not the right word. I like how rhythmic it is and how it helps me drown out the noise in my head."

He made a show of sucking air in over his teeth. "Ok-a-ay…"

She scowled at him. "You know what I mean."

"You have a noisy head."

"Exactly." The word dripped sarcasm. Emma was back. She tossed her hair back over her shoulders as she gave him a challenging look. "You should try knitting."

"Why's that?"

"Keep you from worrying so much."

"I don't—" She snorted and he shifted course. "I like to plan things out."

"And prepare for every eventuality."

"I quit my job and I'm following the circuit."

"After living in a trailer in a field and saving enough money to provide a decent cushion if this doesn't work out."

"Nothing wrong with that."

"Not one thing," she agreed in a mild tone.

Right. So he shouldn't feel defensive about it. Except living with the fact that his twin was more financially secure than he was, despite his lack of planning, made Jess feel as if he'd been overly cautious.

He hadn't been. He'd been sensible.

"Tyler never had to worry about the future because he had you."

Jess frowned at her. How had she known what he'd been thinking? The fact that she read him so easily bothered him a little.

When they reached the Short Branch, Jess opened the door and a blast of country music hit them hard. Emma showed the bouncer her ID, then squared her shoulders and stepped into the packed bar. Jess put a hand to her side to keep from losing her and felt her muscles tighten. He dropped his hand but followed close behind her as she wound through the crowd to the opposite side of the room where Chase and Dermott sat with a group of rodeo folk.

Having snagged two orphan chairs along the way, he held one out for Em as they settled at the edge of the group. Lara was there, smiling at Dermott as he told a story with a lot of one-armed gestures due to his surgery. She glanced up, saw Jess and her smile widened. And maybe it was his imagination, but he thought he felt Em stiffen beside him.

She and Lara had been competitors once upon a time and, given Lara's prima donna tendencies and Em's penchant for calling things the way she saw them, he could see friction developing between the two.

Chase passed the pitcher of beer their way, along with two empty glasses. "We anticipated your arrival."

Emma smiled at him, then held up her glass, meeting Jess's gaze over the top before she drank. "To a good ride."

She was making amends for giving her honest opinion earlier, and it didn't sit well with him. He liked honesty. He'd just been caught off guard by Em's. "But not the best," he said, even though he didn't yet know if he agreed with her. He'd see if he could find LeClair's ride online. He'd been prepping for his own ride and had missed it.

"What are you talking about?" one of the bronc riders asked. "You had top score."

Jess shot Em a quick look. She raised her eyebrows at him, giving him permission to rat her out, but he just shook his head. "Always looking for improvement," he said. "But your ride, Clancy, that was sheer poetry."

"Damn straight." The bronc rider lifted his glass and drank deeply.

IT'D BEEN A long time since Emma had been out. Darion wasn't fond of crowds or loud parties, and after Len had died, she'd preferred to stay at home. But tonight, for the first time in a long time, being in the crowded bar made her feel energized instead of isolated. Another step forward.

She glanced over at Jess, glad that he'd pushed her to come with him, and met Lara's gaze. Even though she did her best to fight it, there was something about the woman that rubbed her wrong, so she lifted an eyebrow and purposely shifted in her chair so she was closer to Jess. He turned toward her, no doubt surprised that her shoulder had bumped his, but she only smiled. Lara could see the smile. She couldn't see Jess's perplexed expression, which was probably a good thing.

"Everything okay?" he asked.

"Fine," she said lightly. She wasn't normally a person who played games, but Lara and Jess had broken up over a year ago and she didn't appreciate being treated as if she were encroaching on Lara's territory.

The looks continued and Emma stayed parked right where she was, close to Jess's side. He was sturdy and warm, and when he laughed, she liked the way his body moved. He put a hand on the back of her chair at one point, seemingly unaware of the way it brought them even closer, focused as he was on another of Dermott's hilarious stories. On the other side of the table, Lara held court, but she was watching Jess. Watching Em. It was getting old and she was debating about whether or not to address the issue when Jess nudged her. "Close?"

Len's phrase. He'd never bothered asking if a person was close to leaving. Instead it was simply, "Close?"

Emma's throat tightened a little as she nodded. She was ready to roll out her bed in the back seat of the truck and conk out. They had a four-hour drive ahead of them the next morning and would be up at the crack of dawn.

"It's time." She pushed back her chair and got to her feet.

"I'll walk with you guys," Lara said brightly, also rising.

"So will I." Chase pulled his wallet out and fished for a tip.

"I figured you'd shut the place down," Dermott grumbled to his friend.

"Too many miles tomorrow." Chase set a five on the table. "But feel free to shut it down for me."

Dermott let out a breath and pulled his own wallet out. The place was rocking and their table was commandeered almost before they were all to their feet.

"Are we getting old?" Chase asked after as they'd woven their way through the crowd and emerged in the much quieter street. The carnival lights were still on, but the rides were still.

"Never." But there wasn't a lot of conviction in Dermott's voice. Chase and Dermott guys were close to thirty. Jess was thirty. Rough stock riding was a young man's sport, which, she knew, was why Jess had finally broken free of his self-imposed life rules and regulations and given his first love the attention it deserved. That took guts, and Emma was impressed that he was actually doing what he'd talked about doing forever. He belonged on the pro circuit with his twin, because in Emma's mind, he was better than Tyler. More consistent. More studied and exact in his approach to the sport.

Somehow Lara had managed to fall in step with Jess, so Emma walked between Chase and Dermott.

When they parted ways at the field where the competitors parked their trucks and trailers, Lara took Jess aside. Emma gave a mental shrug and started for the truck. She didn't like the woman. She really didn't. However, whatever went on between Lara and Jess... was none of her business.

She was reminding herself of that fact when the truck lights flashed and she turned to see Jess jogging to catch up with her.

"Escaped, I see." He frowned at her as she pulled open the door. "Never mind."

He rubbed a hand over his forehead. "You know... just because you think it, you don't *have* to say it."

She smiled at him over her shoulder. "Well aware. Because otherwise I would have told Lara to stop with the laser eyes." She held up her hand, the tips of her thumb and forefinger separated by a fraction of an inch. "I was this close before the party broke up."

Jess snorted. "Might be a good thing we left."

"I'm not in the mood to deal with Lara's delusions on top of everything else."

He pulled in a long breath and rested a hand on the cab of the truck, effectively closing her in, making her suddenly all that more aware of him, and she wondered if he knew what he was doing.

"Yet you encouraged those delusions."

She angled her chin at him. "What do you mean?"

"I mean that you're competitive and so is she. And I was stuck in between you two tonight."

She felt heat in her cheeks as his meaning became clear. "You think that I was treating you like a prize to be won?"

"Maybe."

"Jess—"

"Lara and I are done. She knows that. But she likes attention and she likes to win. You were all but waving a red flag at her tonight."

"It wasn't because of you."

"It was because you like to win, too."

Emma let out a frustrated breath and studied the ground. He was right. Even if he wasn't, she wanted to continue this journey and arguing with Jess wasn't going to further her goal. "Okay. Maybe you have a point."

"Maybe?"

Humble pie time. "I won't mess with Lara again. And I appreciate you asking me to come with you. I haven't been out much since Len died, and I enjoyed tonight, despite Lara."

A shadow crossed his face. "You and Darion never went out?"

"Not with a raucous group. I didn't feel like it and Darion—"

"Is quiet. I know."

She glanced down at the toe of her bright red boot. She didn't want to discuss Darion. Time to change topics again. "What time will you be banging on the window tomorrow?"

"Around five."

Five hours of sleep? Probably more like four because she had things to work over in her head. She could handle it. "See you then."

Jess gave her a long look, a look that sent an odd shiver through her middle, and even though he didn't move, she felt as if he'd somehow gotten closer. "Right."

He still wasn't moving, and she was about to ask him what the deal was when he lowered his hand from the side of the truck and lightly cupped the side of her face.

"Thanks for not taking Lara down in the bar."

He casually dropped his hand back to his side and, even though it was nothing—just a friendly touch—it felt different than when he'd touched her leg in the bar to get her attention, or when she'd leaned closer to him for effect.

"Anytime, Jess. Now honestly. I have to get some sleep."

JESS COULD STILL feel a slight tingle in his fingertips from where he'd touched Emma's cheek as he walked to the rear of the truck. A small caress, meant as a gesture of solidarity, but from the way her eyes had widened when he made contact, it was obvious she hadn't taken it that way.

And it hadn't felt that way.

He let out a sigh. Nothing was ever easy with Emma. He'd have to straighten this out later. Explain his intentions...

Or not.

Knowing Emma, it would only make things worse. Best to leave well enough alone and avoid touching her in the future.

He opened the camper and climbed inside, hung his hat on the hook next to the door, shrugged out of his clothes and crawled into his bunk in his underwear. No going commando on this trip—just in case he was called into action in the middle of the night.

He stretched out on the mattress, still feeling bad about Emma sleeping in the cramped back seat. He was too tall for the truck seat and she was too...Emma...to be in the camper with him. He'd never get any sleep.

And after what had just happened...

He flopped over on his back.

At least Em hadn't taken Lara on in the bar. Lara was spoiled and she wanted him, but only because *he'd* broken things off with *her*, instead of it being the other way around. Like he'd told Emma, Lara didn't like losing. She wanted another round so that *she* could walk away first.

Wasn't going to happen.

He stared up at the ceiling. Had LeClair really won the day? He didn't think so, but even if Tim had won, Jess had been in the money, which he needed to do—consistently—if he was going to reach his goal.

And if you don't?

He'd saved a healthy amount of money by living in a camp trailer on an old homestead site in a field, so he had enough to tide him over until he found a new job.

If things got really tight, he could move the trailer onto Ty and Skye's place—although he'd rather not do that. He was the responsible twin, after all. What would it look like if Tyler started rescuing him?

Ty would love it.

Jess would not. He snapped on the dim bunk light and pulled his small notebook out of the cubby above his head and opened it to the goals page. He was a goal-writer, much to his twin's delight. Nothing Ty had liked better than to find his brother's notebook and see what Jess had planned for his life. Ty's goals had been more short-term and shoot-from-the-hip—things like survive the ride, party till dawn.

His goals were relatively simple for the next few months—win enough money to make the finals, keep expenses down, avoid getting hurt. He hadn't written the last goal down, but it was always in his head. He turned to the last expense page, where he'd noted the amounts he had budgeted in one column and the actual amounts spent in another. So far, so good. If he kept this up, he'd be ahead of the game.

All was well.

He closed the book, tucked it away, shut off the light and rolled over onto his side, shifting his bruised leg to a more comfortable position. And the first thought that drifted into his head was the look on Emma's face when he'd touched her cheek.

So much for being distracted by reviewing his plans and goals. This Emma thing... It was not working out the way he thought it was going to, and he was going to have to watch himself.

Len wouldn't have liked it if Jess messed with his little sister.

JESS WAS QUIET the next morning. He headed out to get coffee and donuts for the drive while she stowed her sleeping bag and other gear in the camper. She locked the door and stripped down to take a quick shower, and when she left the camper, she found him sitting in the driver's seat, the pastries and coffees on the center console beside him. At least that answered the question of who was driving.

"I got the jelly kind you like," he said as he started the engine.

"Thanks."

Emma fastened her seat belt, then retrieved her sunglasses from the dashboard and slipped them onto her nose. She sensed Jess giving her a quick look, but when she glanced his way, he was putting the truck in gear. He maneuvered the vehicle through a narrow space between two horse trailers, then pulled out into the road leading to the highway.

Things felt awkward.

She wasn't going to have it. She'd come along on this trip to be with someone neutral. Someone she trusted who didn't have an active stake in her life or her business. Somehow, four days in, Jess didn't seem so neutral.

He touched you. Big deal. A friendly pat on the cheek.

Only it hadn't been a pat. It'd been a caress. And it had started a slow burn inside of her that had later sparked restless dreams that she couldn't quite remember.

But what she did remember made her shift in her seat.

Dear heavens. She cleared her throat, drawing Jess's attention. Enough of this.

"I just wanted to let you know that I don't care if Lara shoots daggers at me."

"Why did you care last night?"

"I don't know. Maybe the beer? I don't drink much." She reached for her coffee, took a sip and burned her tongue. "And sorry for telling you she wasn't done with you. None of my business."

He didn't answer and when she chanced a glance, he seemed to be mulling over her words.

She faced forward again feeling weary, even though the sun had barely shown above the horizon. "You know, when I was younger, all I wanted to do was to belong. To have the Laras of the world welcome me as one of their own. I still might harbor a touch of resentment toward her kind for not accepting me."

"Why?" He seemed genuinely perplexed.

"It's important to belong. You had Tyler. You were never alone. I had a bunch of younger brothers who wanted to play army, and an older brother who was hell-bent on protecting me and leaving me behind while he had fun. My friends, Cynthia and Robbie, wanted to belong as much as I did. So we'd talk. Plot how to break into the inner circle."

She leaned her head back against the seat and chanced another sip of coffee. Better. The caffeine started rolling through her system, making her feel more like herself. Or maybe it was because the after-effects of the dreams were evaporating now that she was more awake.

"You know what I think of when I think of the inner circle?"

"What?" She gave him a curious look.

"They're a bunch of fancy show horses that can't

hack it out on the range where it counts." He pulled out onto the highway and maneuvered into position behind a pickup going his speed.

"Not all of them were show horses," Emma said. "Some of those people were simply comfortable in their skin." She adjusted her glasses, which had slipped down her nose. "I was comfortable enough with my friends— but when I was around the chosen few, I felt like I had four eyes or something." She gave him a dark look. "Maybe something to do with people teasing me about my mouth."

"You grew into it."

"What?"

"Your mouth. Looks good now."

She gave him an exasperated look. "That doesn't help salve the wounds of high school."

"Were you that wounded?"

She thought for a moment. "I didn't like being teased. But…no. I was tough." A sigh escaped her lips. "I did want to be popular."

Jess's hand moved in her direction, almost as if he was going to pat her shoulder, then it abruptly shifted course and he grabbed his coffee.

"Careful," she said. "It's hot."

"Thanks." He kept his eyes on the road and the atmosphere in the truck edged toward uncomfortable. Em shifted in her seat. This was getting weird.

"What's happening?"

Jess's gaze jerked toward her. "What do you mean?"

"You know what I mean. Why are things between us…different?"

She thought he was going to say that they weren't, but instead he muttered, "Maybe because you grew into your mouth." Emma blinked at him. He shrugged without looking at her. "You've changed. I've changed. Guess we need to get used to that."

"Right." She gave her head a small shake and grimaced at the highway.

They had changed. But she wasn't going to let it matter, because if it did matter—too much—Jess would cut her trip short and she'd be back at the motel, dodging Selma.

Although…it would probably take her a few days to realize her stepdaughter was back in town…

No. She preferred being on the road with Jess. When she went back, she'd have it out with Selma once and for all.

As if that would work.

She put her coffee back in the holder, folded her arms and closed her eyes. She hadn't gotten a lot of rest the night before. "Don't watch me while I sleep," she murmured without opening her eyes.

She heard Jess give a small snort of acknowledgment. "Wouldn't dream of it," he replied.

And speaking of dreams, she really hoped she didn't have any.

Chapter Seven

During her barrel racing days, the Red Lodge Rodeo had been one of Emma's favorites, and she felt a pang as they drove past the Welcome to Red Lodge sign. She had no intention of running barrels again—she couldn't afford the horse or the travel—but a part of her missed the life she'd given up after her brother's death. The hole that had opened up had been so huge and all-consuming that even Selma had shut down. It had taken her days to take up the reins of the family again, and then she'd become even more controlling. Selma's way of dealing with grief.

Jess stopped at a light and Emma gave him a quick look under the guise of checking out a store on the opposite side of the street. He'd lost, too. He and Len had been almost as tight as he and his twin. Tighter in some ways. And she sensed that they were both still raw. If it hadn't been for Len, he wouldn't have brought her along and she would have had to come up with another way to find the space to settle things in her head.

The rodeo started in the early evening. They would spend the night before traveling on to Livingston the next morning for the final day of that rodeo.

"We missed the parade," she said as they drove into

the rodeo grounds, trying to make things feel normal once again. "I'm a parade nerd."

The corners of his mouth lifted. "Imagine that."

"Meaning?"

"You've been in every parade I attended in Gavin."

"I didn't miss many." None that she could recall before she'd graduated high school. Selma had enjoyed dressing her kids in various themed outfits—Emma's favorite was the mounted Smurfs, which her brothers had hated—and heaven help them if another group won the youth trophy. After that it was 4-H, rodeo club, high school homecoming—if there was a parade, she'd been involved.

"We can see the fireworks in Livingston instead," he said as he parked.

She met his gaze as she reached for the door handle. "Sounds good."

Things felt a little better between them. As if he was making as much of an effort to put things back on a normal track as she was. She very much wanted to stay on the same page, so she was going to be the picture of polite cooperation. No more debates about inane topics or giving her opinion on his rides.

She needed to keep an emotional distance—somehow— because this growing awareness of the man was increasingly unsettling. Especially when he did things like mention that her mouth looked good.

Well, his mouth looked good, too, and she shouldn't be noticing. Hadn't she just learned a hard lesson about becoming romantically involved with a guy who'd been her friend?

Yes, she had, and she was not going to make that mistake again.

Jess met her at the front of the truck and handed her the key to the camper. "Would you mind making a couple sandwiches while I check in?"

Emma took the key. "Sure."

"Thanks, kid."

Her old nickname. The one she'd hated when she *was* a kid. The one that reminded her of how he'd treated her and how he probably still thought of her, even if he did think her mouth looked good.

"No problem."

JESS WAS ON the road for one reason—to prove that he was ready to tackle the pro circuit. To address that final bit of doubt as to whether he was ready to give up the security of a full-time job and operate without a safety net—something he'd never done before. He'd envisioned the summer as one of total focus, eye on the prize. What he hadn't envisioned was having Emma ride shotgun, distracting him. And the bitch of it was, she wasn't trying to distract him. Nope—that was entirely on him.

He didn't know what to do about it, except to drag his eye back to that prize, focus on his goal. It was the only way he was going to achieve anything.

If only she hadn't grown into that mouth.

Jess rounded the corner of his camper and stopped just short of running into a guy leading a horse. He blinked at the man, who gave him a frowning look before walking on, and realized just how deep he'd been in his head. And that was a problem, because he was thinking about Em and not about his ride. His rides hadn't suffered because of it—yet. But the season was young.

After the grand entry, he returned to the truck and

stretched while he waited for his event. Considering the number of rodeos he attended, it was amazing how little of them he'd seen. He preferred to spend the time before his event going over the ride. Again and again and again. Tonight he'd drawn Squirrely. The bull had been named for the kink in his broken tail, but his personality reflected his name. He was a tad unpredictable. Jess just hoped he got a decent ride out of him, because he wasn't settling for second place tonight.

When the barrel racing began, Jess headed for the chutes, more focused than he'd been the past two rides. He was ready. He hoped Squirrely was ready, too. He rode last again, which meant that he'd know everyone's scores going in. Not that it mattered—he was not giving less than his best—but it was always good to have a number to shoot for.

As it turned out, that number was eight-nine, which was going to be a challenge.

Jess was ready. More than ready.

Squirrely was ready, too. The bull rolled an eye back at Jess as he climbed on board and adjusted his grip. He shifted his seat on the bull's broad back, found the sweet spot, nodded and the gate flew open. The bull gave a mighty leap out of the chute and then launched into a series of spins, first one way and then the other, and the next thing Jess knew his weight was over his hand, fighting gravity.

As he went off to his left, the rope twisted over his hand, making it impossible to release as he headed toward the ground. He bounced along the side of the bull a couple of times, sweaty hair and muscle grinding into his cheek, then finally got his feet under him and managed to slacken the rope enough to release his hand.

He landed in a heap, but Squirrely wasn't done with him. A bruising kick whooshed by Jess's head and shoulder, just grazing him as he threw himself on the ground again. As soon as Squirrely gave him some room, Jess was up and running for the fence while the bullfighters did their best to distract the bull from his prey.

As soon as he hit the fence, Jess started climbing. Squirrely raced by, now intent on finding the gate instead of punishing his rider. Once he brushed past, Jess got down from the fence and headed for the man gate, waving his hand in acknowledgment as the announcer encouraged the cheering crowd to "pay off this bull rider."

It wasn't until he was out the gate and coiling his bull rope that he realized his shoulder hurt like a son of a gun. Even a grazing kick from a one-ton animal did damage. He said a few words to his fellow competitors as he walked past, congratulated LeClair, who was going to win the event, then headed for the truck. He was almost to the end of the alley behind the chutes when he looked up and saw Emma waiting there, her face paler than usual.

"Don't you usually watch from the stands?"

"I do." She took a few steps forward. "I felt the need to…check on you."

"I'm okay. Wish I would have stayed topside, but… I'm good."

She gave a silent nod and fell in step with him, keeping a little more physical distance than she needed to. "I never asked this before, but what do you do after a ride that doesn't go well?"

"Dissect it and determine to do better next time."

"I meant for your body."

"Oh." He glanced over at her. "Ice. Anti-inflammatories."

"Ever think about turning the truck around and heading home?"

They'd just reached the truck as she spoke, and he reached under the wheel well for the keys that he tucked up there when he wasn't using them, sucking in a pained breath as his shoulder lit on fire. Emma took them from him and unlocked the door.

"That's not one of my strategies for winning."

"Maybe it should be your strategy for not killing yourself. It was scary watching that bull try to take you out."

He blinked at her. This was quite literally not Emma's first rodeo. She knew about bull riding and the risks involved.

"Em, you came along as a driver, not my conscience."

She propped her hands on her hips and pressed her lips together as she held his gaze. And whereas the old Emma would have argued, this Emma remained stonily silent. Which made him feel the need to talk.

He didn't want to.

"I need to ice my shoulder."

"How about your wrist?"

He unbuttoned the cuff and pulled it back. His skin was already turning bluish-black. Emma gave a snort. "Ice that, too."

He leveled a look at her. "You do know that I've done this before, right?"

Her gaze dropped briefly as a wash of color swept across her cheeks. "Right. I…uh… Len. You know?"

He reached out without thinking, putting his sore arm around her and pulled her closer, giving her a brotherly hug while murmuring against her hair, "Yeah. I know. Trust me."

She pulled back a little, a faint frown drawing her eyebrows together as she looked up at him. Her lips trembled as she tried to find words, and that was when Jess gave in to temptation, lowered his head and brought his mouth down to lightly graze hers. Emma went still, and then she slid her hands up his chest and kissed him.

No more wondering what her mouth would feel like beneath his. Perfect. He started to gather her closer, when she pulled back and he immediately loosened his hold. She drew in a small breath as she put space between them.

"Em—"

She raised a hand, cutting him off. "No worries. Really. I've been wondering about this, too." She raised her gaze to meet his dead-on. "Now we know. Right?"

He could see that she desperately needed him to agree. "Right." He smiled a little. "Just a moment of temporary insanity. Happens to the best of us."

"After Darion and everything… You understand?" Did he ever. He shouldn't have kissed her—and more than that, he shouldn't want to kiss her again.

He gave her what he hoped was a reassuring look. "Totally get it." He took her by the shoulders and looked her in the eye. "Forgive me?"

She gave a short scoffing laugh. "Nothing to forgive. Let's just…move on."

"As in pretend it didn't happen?"

"I'm going to give it my best shot."

So was he, but he was beyond certain that his best shot wasn't going to be enough to put that short, sweet kiss out of his head.

WHEN EMMA STARTED her road trip with Jess, she'd fully acknowledged that she was running from trouble instead of dealing with it—and she was okay with that, because she would return to Gavin to fight her battles just as soon as she got a handle on things. The problem was, she was no closer to having a handle on things now than when she'd left. And now she had another facet to deal with—the Jess facet. Dear heavens, but the man could kiss, and it had taken every bit of willpower she had to pull herself away from him last night.

She still half regretted that decision, which was almost as unsettling as the kiss itself.

Emma caught a sigh before it escaped her lips. That was all she needed—to have Jess hear her sighing as she stared off into the distance. He'd insisted on driving, despite his shoulder injury, and she'd acquiesced. One thing she'd learned from growing up with brothers—if a guy was going to insist on being all manly, trying to talk sense was only a waste of breath.

Emma's phone buzzed and Jess glanced her way. Their gazes connected for an electric moment before Emma looked down at her phone and saw her brother's name.

"Wylie," she murmured. "He checks in with me every day." She tapped out a quick answer.

"Nice of him."

Emma cast him a wry look, glad to have a safe topic. "He reports back to Selma. Kind of a double agent."

Jess gave a snort. "At least you know they care about you."

"Care about me. Need to control me." She let the sigh escape this time. "They don't know what to do with me. I'm twenty-five years old, but I honestly believe that Selma thinks if I marry someone, she's done her job. Then she can focus on the boys."

"Lucky boys."

"I know."

Jess maneuvered around a cattle truck. "Why did you want to marry Darion?"

"He was safe." As only a good friend could be.

"Why *didn't* you marry him?"

Emma let a beat of silence pass before saying softly, "He's safe." She pressed her lips together. She wasn't going there. Wasn't going to discuss her ill-fated engagement with Jess—yet another thing she was in the process of figuring out. Jess must have read her vibe, because he adjusted his grip on the steering wheel and leaned back in his seat. Conversation over. Excellent.

They passed a sign indicating that Livingston was only sixteen miles away. After five days and three rodeos, Emma knew the drill. They would arrive at the venue, Jess would head for the rodeo office while she walked off the kinks from the drive. She'd check out the vendor shows and Jess would keep to himself as he eased into competition mode. Jess was a mellow guy—or at least he seemed mellow compared to Tyler—but he was a fierce competitor…which explained why it ticked him off when she'd told him that LeClair should have won two rodeos ago.

After seeing the sights, Emma would read or knit until the rodeo started, then pay her admission and find a seat up high. Some people liked to be close to the action—she liked the nosebleed seats. She was more of a big-picture kind of person, while Jess focused on details. Which was why they drove each other crazy.

Emma waited until they were parked at the rodeo grounds and out of the truck before saying, "If I don't see you before your event, good luck."

He cocked an eyebrow at her. "Big plans?"

"I'm going to keep myself entertained." As in she would find a quiet place, where she wasn't distracted by his presence, and text her brother. Find out what the deal was with Selma, whom Wylie said was acting strange—well, stranger than usual. He was concerned. And she wondered if this was a ruse to get her back home. If they needed her back home for a legitimate reason, she would go. If Selma just needed to continue on her path of total domination, then she was staying right where she was. With Jess. At least the problem with Jess was manageable, since they were on the same page. It wasn't exactly comfortable riding with him after knowing what his mouth felt like on hers, but she could deal. She'd be careful about how she offered—or accepted—condolences and comfort.

JESS DIDN'T SEE Em again before the rodeo started, which was better for his concentration. How could he not be distracted? He now knew what Em's lips felt like, tasted like, and he could still vividly recall the soft intake of breath as his mouth had settled on hers. She'd been startled, but she'd kissed him back.

And now she was totally withdrawn. There'd been no arguing or banter on the two-hour drive between Red Lodge and Livingston. Only silence, broken on occasion by a comment on passing scenery—just enough talk to allow them to pretend that it was business as usual. But it wasn't. They were both working through what had happened and, Jess hoped, coming to the same conclusion. The kiss might have been inevitable, but it was done and not to be repeated. Eventually they would fall back into their old roles.

Right around the time pigs flew.

Because he wasn't thinking of her as Len's little sister anymore. Good or bad, things had changed between them. Len would have beat the crap out of him if he'd known the direction Jess's thoughts were taking during the occasional weak moment.

"Hey, Doublemint." A hand clapped him on the back, but Jess didn't need to turn to know that it was Wes Fremont.

"Wes. How's it going?" Obnoxious Wes was back after having been put out of action the first rodeo of the season.

"Ready to ride." He smirked. "Still trying to catch up with your brother?"

"Still as unpleasant as ever?" Jess asked mildly.

Wes laughed. "I gotta be me." He tipped his hat back as he looked out over the stands as if searching for someone. "I heard that Emma Sullivan is traveling with you."

"How do you know Em?"

Wes snorted. "She was, like, the hottest thing going when she chased those cans."

"Really?" Jess's tone sounded deadly, even to his own ears, but he wasn't having a jerk like Wes sniffing around Em. Not when she was still piecing things back together anyway.

Wes instantly lifted his hands. "Hey, I thought you were only traveling together. That's what Lara told me."

"Lara's right," Jess said abruptly. The tractor that had been leveling the arena in preparation for the barrel racing shifted gears as it roared through the gate. Jess gave Wes a pointed look. "You're up first, right?"

Wes smirked again, taking the hint. "I am. Wish me luck?"

"Nothing but."

After Wes moved on, Jess scanned the packed bleachers for Em, but it didn't take long for him to give it up as hopeless. He turned back toward the alley where Wes was now in deep conversation with another bull rider. He needed to put Em out of his head. Concentrate on the reason he was there.

Which seemed to be becoming more difficult with each passing day.

HE WAS UP third on the roster and was prepping his bull rope when the last barrel time was announced. The animal he'd drawn, Boston B., was unknown to him—a new bull to the contractor and he was the animal's first official ride.

The bull was unusually quiet in the chute, but Jess had had many bulls that faked a calm disposition before letting all hell fly once the gate opened. As it turned out, Boston wasn't faking. Not on that night anyway. When the gate opened he gave a halfhearted rear out into the arena and then began a few lazy spins. To change things up, and to make certain that Jess didn't get a re-ride due to the bull's sorry performance, he ended with a spin in the opposite direction and a couple of decent high bucks. Stuff that practice bulls did for beginning riders.

Jess dismounted, landed on his feet, nodded his appreciation to the crowd, then marched to the gate, his jaw muscles clenched tight.

His fault yesterday. The bull's fault today. He wouldn't be in the money unless everyone else got bucked off, and that didn't happen. When the event ended, it was bull riders six, bulls four. He was one of the six who'd stayed on, but his score was at the bottom. Thank you, Boston.

He headed back to the truck as soon as the event was over, fighting frustration. He was about to smack his hat on his leg when a voice sounded from behind him.

"Sorry about your ride."

He turned to see Lara bearing down on him. "It happens."

"Yeah. I know, but it's still rough." She caught up with him and gave him a rueful smile. "Same thing happened to me tonight. Donovan wasn't on and I got fifth. Won't even pay my gas."

He nodded, feeling a little cold as he did so, but frankly, all he wanted was to be alone, and if he commiserated…well…he wouldn't be. They were almost to the truck when Lara said, "A few of us are going out tonight, if you'd like to join us." He started to shake his head and she added, "Emma can come along, too…if you want."

He stopped walking. "We have a long drive tomorrow." And he rather doubted he would see Em, who was going to watch the crowning of the queen and the fireworks from the stands. He planned to have an early night and go over a few things—like tapes of the bull he'd pulled at the Coyote Creek Roundup in two days.

"Suit yourself," Lara said lightly before reaching out to lightly pat his vest. She remained focused on the cen-

ter of his chest for a moment, then gave him an appraising look. And that was when he realized that as far as
she was concerned, things were not done between them.

Excellent.

He forced a smile. "Have a good night, Lara." He
turned and headed for the back of the truck. By the time
he got the door unlocked, she was on her way back toward the stands, where she was probably meeting up
with friends.

Once inside the camper, he shucked out of his vest
and chaps, jeans and shirt, and put on sweatpants and
a T-shirt. There were shouts and whoops going on outside and in the distance he heard the first pops of fireworks, but he didn't care. He was done for the day. His
big season wasn't panning out so well. Bull riding was
a big-picture sport, but two bad rides in a row left him
feeling edgy.

Next ride would be better. He'd just pulled up the
videos of Scavenger, his next draw, when there was a
light tap on the door.

"It's open," he called from the bunk.

The door swung open and Em stuck her head inside.
"Come and watch the fireworks," she said.

"I'm not exactly dressed for it."

"Yeah. Like people are going to be offended by
sweatpants."

He scowled at her, then swung his legs out of the
bunk. "I was watching a video."

"I'll drive tomorrow. You can burn up data then."

"Is there a reason you're so hell-bent on me watching fireworks?"

"Yeah," she said simply. "Maybe I want us to do

things together like friends instead of dealing with this full-time awkwardness."

Oh, man. His expression softened. "You can't force some things, Em. They are what they are."

She stared at him for a moment. "Maybe you could expand that answer."

He studied her face, knew exactly what she wanted him to tell her. And it wouldn't be true. Things were no longer the way they once were between them. "Do you really want me to?"

Color washed over her cheeks. "Maybe not. But I don't want to feel uncomfortable for the rest of this trip."

"You can go home anytime you want."

"Do you want me to go home?"

"I'd like to be able to concentrate."

Her chin came up. "Are you saying that I'm keeping you from concentrating?" Her expression shifted. "Wait a minute…are you blaming me for your bad rides?"

"That would be handy," he said patiently, "but no. That's on me."

"But I disrupt your concentration."

"I think about you." The honest truth. "And to be honest, I don't think I'll be able to put you back into the little sister niche."

"How about the friend niche?" she asked in a low voice.

"I can try."

"Try?"

He got up off the bunk and Emma stepped back onto the ground from where she'd been perched on the fold-down steps, allowing him a path out of the camper. A couple of cowboys drifted by as Jess stepped out onto the grass. He nodded at them and one of them raised a hand in acknowledgment. When he looked back at Emma, her mouth was tight, her posture stiff. Behind her an explosion of pink and blue lit the sky. She didn't so much as flinch.

"I'm not trying to make your life more difficult," he said.

"You're failing."

"You kissed me back the other night."

He could tell by the way her eyes went wide that she hadn't expected him to address the true cause of their mutual discomfort. That wasn't the way he did things, and, until now, he didn't think it was the way that Em did things either.

"Maybe I did…and maybe I regret it."

"No. Obviously you regret it."

"Jess…" She made a frustrated gesture. "It was one kiss. Just…a kiss."

Which was all it had taken for him to start to see her differently.

"Look—I'm not asking for more. I'm just explaining why things may never feel the same between us. I'll do my thing and you'll do yours and we can ride to these rodeos together, but the fact of the matter is that things have changed, and they'll probably get more comfortable with time…but right now…"

Her lips parted, but no words came out. Unusual for Em. She turned away as another burst of color lit the sky. Green, followed by white, followed by red. When she turned back she had her determined face on. The one that used to mean trouble for him.

"We can move past this."

He nodded. "I don't see that we have a lot of choice."

"I just broke my engagement. I'm not about to mess up my life again."

"Because we both know what a screwup I am. Irresponsible. Never having a plan."

She took a step back, her face going pale. "What are you saying, Jess?"

He reached out and hooked a finger in her belt, easing her a few steps closer. She did not fight him, which said a lot. "Do I have to spell it out?"

"No," she said abruptly. "Do not spell." She stepped back so that his hand fell away. But he still felt the connection. "This is not how I saw things playing out."

"You mean—"

"I mean," she said, cutting him off as if being afraid of what he might articulate, "that I thought we would sit on the grass and watch the fireworks and start easing back into the way things were." She stuck her chin out. "You're not playing along."

"Don't feel like playing, Em. I feel like being honest."

"If we…took a chance and it didn't work out…I would lose you forever."

"Lose me? Or your connection to Len?"

"Maybe both." She took a step back, hugging herself in a way that made him want to take her into his arms and make things better. But he couldn't do that.

"I don't want to take that kind of chance." Not yet anyway. "So don't worry about that."

"Then what *do* you want?"

"To tell you the truth, Em, I don't know right now."

"Well, that's a lot of help." She took a pace and then turned back, jumping as more fireworks went off. "So I'll tell you what we're going to do. We're going to pretend. I'll live with the fact that I'm going to feel uncomfortable for a while, and you can live with me being a distraction."

He tucked a thumb into the pocket of his sweats. "Are you sure you don't want to go home?"

"No. I'm not running twice. I'll see this out and then go home and deal with Selma."

Chapter Eight

Why couldn't Jess have simply remained her friendly nemesis?

Emma swallowed yet another sigh as she finished one row of knitting and started the next. Life would have been so much easier. She kept her eyes on her knitting, as she always did when she wasn't driving, and Jess focused on the road, but that didn't keep him from distracting her in a way that was beginning to wear on her patience.

All she wanted was independence, but her quest for autonomy wasn't going well, because of the man sitting a few feet away from her, looking good, smelling great. Ignoring her.

Good. She wanted to be ignored. She wasn't ready to go home, but she didn't want to deal with the situation she was sliding into. Besides, Jess had hit the nail on the head when he said that she was not only afraid of losing him as a friend, but of also losing her connection to Len. Jess had known her brother in a way no one else had, and when she was near Jess, she might feel Len's loss a little more, but she also felt as if she was closer to him. Jess was a connection. A partner in grieving. Other than her reclusive father, no one missed Len more than the two of them.

Here she was, edging back into Darion territory. He had been a rock while she grieved. But she'd mistaken closeness, safety and security for more intense feelings. As had he.

Great guy, Darion.

Not the guy for her. And because of their mistake, the friendship would never be the same. He was now chilling in Kalispell and she was hiding from her stepmom on the rodeo circuit. The last time she'd spoken to him had been shortly after their breakup, and when he'd left, she'd had no one to bounce things off. It wasn't as if Wylie was going to be a lot of help, being a know-it-all eighteen-year-old who was afraid of his mother.

Ah, Darion. Her needles stilled. She regretted the loss, but knew in her heart that the rift would never be fully mended.

She managed a sideways look at Jess without him noticing. His gaze was on the road, but she had no doubt that his head was deep into his next ride. He had the most excellent profile. Model material. She could so envision his face staring out of a magazine ad for, well, just about anything.

She started knitting again, one corner of her mouth lifting as she thought about how that assessment would sit with Mr. Hayward. Not well. Jess avoided the limelight, unless he happened to be on a bull. Then he was a rock star—the embodiment of grit, determination and fearlessness. She loved to watch him ride.

Maybe a little too much, and she needed to keep that in check.

"Good driving."

Emma looked up in time to see a big red Chevy truck cut in front of them after passing on the two-lane road.

"Bronc rider," Emma murmured.

"Probably."

They were part of a long line of traffic heading toward Coyote Creek, now only a few short miles away. The Coyote Creek Roundup was a big deal. The quiet town normally boasted a population of around six thousand, but swelled by another third during its two-day rodeo. There was no secret about what had made the event so popular—a traveling reporter had written an article for a national magazine describing the quaintness of both the event and the venue. After that, people who wanted to experience an event that hadn't gone totally commercial flocked to the area. The result? The event was now totally commercial. But it brought big money into a small ranching community and everyone still seemed to have a good time. And Emma intended to do the same while she was there. She was going to take back control of her life.

When they pulled off the freeway, Emma reached around to the back seat and got her purse.

"Would you drop me downtown?" Jess shot her a perplexed look. "I want to shop for a while. Check out the summer sales at the gift shops."

"I thought you were low on funds."

"Thus the sale part."

Jess maneuvered the truck through the packed streets. "You want me to wait for you? We have a little time before I have to be there."

"Thanks, but I'll walk to the fairgrounds." The exercise would do her good after all the time spent in the truck.

"You know the way?"

Emma let out a long sigh. "Jess. The town is small and I'm not eleven. Just stop the truck and let me out. Okay?"

He did just that, finding a loading zone to pull into.

"I never said you were eleven." She gave him a sardonic look and he had the good grace to shift in his seat. "Fine." Emma opened the door. "Sorry."

The apology surprised her. She accepted it with a short nod and closed the door, lifting her hand to him before turning and heading down the street to the shops.

She worked her way through several, keeping her budget in mind, but picking up a few necessities along the way. She was looking though a display of sale shirts when she heard her name.

No. She couldn't have.

"Emma!"

She turned at the sound of the familiar voice. "Mallory!" Her bag slid up her arm as she closed the distance and gave her friend a hug. "Are you here for the rodeo?"

Mallory shook her head as she stepped back. "Yes and no. I bought a little place fifty miles west of here, so I'm kind of in the area. Kait's barrel racing today."

"I had no idea." Mallory and her sister, Kaitlyn, had lived in Gavin before their parents moved prior to Mallory's and Emma's senior year.

"Well, I kind of dropped out of sight for a while." Mallory's smile wavered for a split second, then came back full force. "Are you here for the rodeo?"

"I'm traveling with Jess Hayward."

"Jess Hayward?" Mallory's eyes widened. "You're traveling with *Jess* Hayward?"

"It's not like that."

"Why not?" Mallory fanned herself. "I haven't seen the guy in ten years and I still recall how hot he was." She narrowed her eyes. "He didn't get ugly did he?"

Hardly. "I needed some space and Jess needed a driver, so I came along for this leg of the circuit."

Mallory frowned at her. "Selma?"

"Got it in one." Emma grinned. She and Mallory might have lost touch, but they'd known each other well at one time. "Will you be around for the rodeo? I'd love to catch up."

"As if happens, I will be, as will Kaitlyn. We can make a night of it."

"You have no idea how much I need a night out."

"Frustration?" Mallory asked with an ironic lift of her eyebrows. Emma gave her a warning look. She wasn't about to let Mallory get started. "Kait and I were going to the Road House after the rodeo."

"Sounds like fun, but I'm on foot."

"Not a problem. Kait has her truck, and she's nuts about it, so I promise that she'll be a safe ride coming and going."

"I'd have to get back early. Day and a half drive to the next rodeo."

"Don't you worry, Cinderella. We'll have you back." She cocked her head. "I, uh, don't suppose that Prince Charming would like to come along?"

"I could ask him."

Mallory smiled. "Why don't you do that?"

EMMA DID NOT ask Jess to accompany her to the Road House with Mallory and Kait. She wanted a relaxing evening out—or maybe she wanted a wild evening out; she wasn't yet certain—and having Jess along would not be conducive to her having a good time. Therefore, she'd left him a note on the door of the camper telling him she was going out after the rodeo and considered matters settled.

Mallory met her near the ticket booth as planned and they bought hot dogs and beer before finding seats near the top of the stands. After the steer wrestling, Mallory pointed out Kaitlyn, who was warming up a sleek liver chestnut in preparation for her barrel run, which wouldn't occur for almost an hour. And there, also warming up nearby, was Emma's favorite winner/ whiner, Lara Wynam. She sincerely hoped that Kait beat Lara today, although, watching Kait's horse dance and whirl, she wondered.

"Girl's a bundle of nerves," Mallory said as her sister pulled her horse to a sliding stop. "And her horse is the same. I don't think anybody but Kait could ride that beast."

"Ever try?"

Mallory slanted her a sideways look. "Kait doesn't like to share." She smiled. "Which works well because I want nothing to do with Mercury."

They continued catching up as they watched the events, Mallory explaining how she'd gotten involved with the wrong guy and had spent years dodging him until finally he disappeared. She now felt safe enough to settle so she had bought the small horse property west of Coyote Creek and Kaitlyn moved in with her to help with payments.

Em's story felt tame by comparison, except for the part about losing her brother. High school graduation, followed by college. She'd dropped out when Len was killed and gave up barrel racing. She and her close friend, Darion, decided to tie the knot and then she realized that she didn't want to marry a friend.

"No spark?" Mallory asked.

An image of Jess flashed in her mind as she shook her head. Now, that was a spark—but the wrong kind.

"Not enough. We had a strong base for a relationship, as long as I was happy with a long un-bumpy road."

"There's a lot to be said for that." Mallory pushed her hair back with both hands, as if brushing away unwanted thoughts. "Take it from one who's had bumps." She gave Em a rueful smile. "You've had a few, too. Just dealing with Selma qualifies. Remember when she wanted you to wear that awful taffeta skirt to prom?"

"Oh, yeah." It'd been her junior year and the popular dress style had been sleek mermaid. Selma had her heart set on Em wearing a taffeta skirt Selma had bought to wear to a community function. The function had been canceled and the skirt never worn. Prom was the perfect place to give it an outing. Em cringed a little at the memory. In high school things like wearing your stepmother's castoffs mattered—as did the fact that the skirt was wildly out of fashion. Again, a huge issue at the age of sixteen.

"I agree." Em sat a little straighter as a tie-down roper made an amazing catch, then tripped as he got off his horse. Poor guy.

"Is Jess coming to the Road House tonight?"

Em met Mallory's gaze. "No." She'd learned long ago while dealing with Selma that a simple no, without explanation, often deflected both questions and arguments.

Mallory frowned, but as Emma had hoped, didn't ask if he'd been invited. He hadn't been because Em didn't want him there. She wasn't ready to hang with him in that kind of setting—at least not until she got her head together. Although…perhaps she'd made a mistake. If he joined them, he'd probably be surrounded by women, like, say, Mallory, and that would be a big step toward her getting a grip.

Huh. "I'll text him after the rodeo. See how he feels."

"Excellent."

Although now that she'd promised, Em wasn't certain how she felt about having her friend possibly hook up with her bull rider—even if he wasn't really *her* bull rider.

"WHAT'S THE REAL deal with you and Emma Sullivan?"

Jess dropped his foot from the rail he'd been using to stretch his tight hamstring before his ride and turned toward Wes Fremont with a deep frown. "What's it to you?"

The cowboy gave a casual shrug. "I don't want to step on toes, but if you're only traveling together, and not involved in a—" he made air quotes "—'secret' relationship, then…" The rise of his eyebrows said the rest.

Emma was no rookie when it came to shutting down cowboys. She'd traveled the circuit for years, barrel racing on both her college team and during the summers, but Jess hated the idea of Wes hitting on her. Hated it a lot. "We're still working that out."

"So nothing definite."

"Leave her alone." There was steel beneath his civil tone.

"What I see here is a case of Emma being able to make her own decisions because you guys aren't really involved." Wes's eyebrows came together in a thoughtful frown. "Although…I think that would be the case no matter what you'd worked out. Em always struck me as one who felt free to go her own way."

Jess considered telling Wes what would happen to him if he didn't stay away from Emma, but the guy had just made a decent point. She was free to go her own way, and she could handle herself. This wasn't his business.

Much.

She was still traveling with him. And even if he no longer saw her in little sister mode, he felt the deep need to watch out for her. She was his travel partner.

And you're falling for her.

The thought slammed into him like a wayward bullet. He was falling for Emma.

This was *not* part of his master plan. Jess gave himself a mental shake. No matter what, he was going to have to deal with it, and the first order of business was to make certain Wes left her alone.

"Em's going through a rough spot. Leave her be."

Wes smirked at him. "Maybe she can tell me about it." The announcer called the first bull rider and Wes took a backward step. "Thanks for the info."

"Leave her be," Jess repeated. Another smirk and Wes turned his back, heading for the other end of the alley.

Jess reached back to fasten the chap straps behind his thighs as Scavenger was loaded, sucked in a breath, prepared to do his job. The animal's neck was slick with sweat when Jess climbed on board several minutes later, the sharp smell stinging his nostrils as he wrapped the rope and gave it a couple of quick pounds. Scavenger was one of those bulls that loved to buck, and from what

Jess had seen, he was fairly set in his patterns—or he had been set until the moment the gate opened and he charged out instead of rearing as he had done in every video clip Jess had watched. Two bounds later he reared sharply then punched the ground with his hind legs, twisting wildly in the air. And that was when Jess's weight shifted and he found himself fighting the laws of physics, trying to stay on board the now-spinning animal while gravity tugged at him.

He hit the ground face-first, a classic dirt sandwich, and stars flashed as he scrambled back to his feet. But unlike Squirrely, Scavenger had no interest in trying to take him out. The bull's job was done and he headed for the gate. Jess's rope fell off just as the animal exited and one of the gate men picked it up, handing it to him as he went by.

He became aware of the crowd, which was paying him off with applause, offering him condolences. He waved then ducked through the gate, a disquieting feeling building inside. For the first time ever, he'd felt something other than stone-cold determination when he climbed on that bull. Had Wes managed to psych him out by talking about hitting on Em?

He reached back to undo the straps behind his thighs and headed down the alley, his loose chaps flapping around his legs. He continued on to the truck, his chin tucked close to his chest as he fought disappointment and anger. When he got to the truck, there was a slip of paper lodged in the door. He pulled it out, unfolded it and read. Looked like he'd have the evening to himself, because Emma was heading to the Road House after the rodeo for drinks with Mallory and Kaitlyn

Flynn. Fine. It would give him time to figure out what had happened with his ride.

Or better yet—he wiped a hand across his grimy face—time to find the showers. Coyote Creek rodeo grounds doubled as a campground and had public shower facilities, so he wouldn't have to hose down in the tiny camper shower stall. That's what he needed. A shower. A beer. An early night…waiting for Em to come home.

He gathered his gear and headed for the showers as the cars started pulling out of the parking lot. The point leaders had been announced, the rodeo was over for the day. The champions would be named tomorrow, but his name wouldn't be mentioned.

Next rodeo.

He undressed slowly, peeled off the tape on his wrist, then found a stall, cranked on the water and put his filthy face directly into the spray. When he finally lowered his chin and opened his eyes, the last of the arena dirt was swirling around his feet and disappearing down the drain. He sincerely hoped his recent losing streak was also heading down the drain. Not since his junior days had he had such a run of bad luck.

He turned and stood under the pounding water, letting it soothe his tight muscles, drum the thoughts out of his brain. Eventually he reached for the soap, lathered up, rinsed off. When he opened the curtain a few minutes later, the place was empty. Apparently he was the only camper who'd taken a dirt bath that night.

As he left the cinder-block building, towel slung around his neck, a big red chromed-out Chevy with a six-inch lift drove by on its way out of the parking lot. The same truck that had cut in front of him on the highway. Jess gave his head a shake. Wes drove a truck that a twelve-year-old would kill for.

Some guys grew up. Some didn't.

The truck rolled to a stop at the end of the parking lot, then pulled out, heading east. Two blocks later it turned onto the street leading to the Road House and disappeared around a corner.

Coincidence that Wes was heading where Emma was?

It didn't matter. Coincidence or not, both he and Em would be there, and he was not going to sit in his bunk, drinking beer while Wes chased after his travel partner.

Chapter Nine

The last time Emma had been in the Road House was shortly after she'd reached legal drinking age and she'd gone out with rodeo buddies to celebrate her best barrel time ever. They'd ended up shutting the place down and the end of the evening was nothing more than a fuzzy memory. As she and Mallory and Kait walked into the crowded bar, she didn't know if she still had the stamina to shut a place down, but she was going to give it a shot.

The Road House was on the peripheries of the small town, more run-down than the other three drinking establishments in Coyote Creek. A favorite of the rodeo crowd, but not so popular with the fans who came into the town for the big event. The other bars were calculatedly quaint and charming and worked to stay that way. The Road House was the same as it'd been for the past three decades. No rugged logs or timbers or leather sofas or animal heads on the wall. "Look! A table," Kait said, pointing across the room.

"Quick—before those guys get it." Mallory slipped past the crowd standing near the door with Emma close behind her. They laughed as they fell into the sturdy wooden barrel chairs, claiming their prize just before the three cowboys who'd also been heading for the table.

"Well played, ladies." One of the guys smiled and winked at Kait. "We might be back," he said before turning to follow his buddies toward the bar.

"I'll get the drinks," Kait said, "if you save my seat, as in, keep an eye on it." She leveled a hard look at her sister, who gave a dismissive wave.

"There are two chairs, if you didn't notice. The chances of someone stealing both are—"

"Excellent, judging from past experience," Kait snapped. She turned to Em. "Watch my chair."

"Will do."

The Road House was full, but it wasn't yet bursting at the seams as it had been the last time Em closed the place down. Tonight she could actually see across the room. She leaned back in her chair and scanned the crowd. She spotted Chase at the bar, standing a few feet away from Kait, who was waiting her turn to order drinks, but she didn't see his travel buddy, Dermott.

Lara was there with a group of barrel racers, sitting at a table on the opposite side of the room. The cowboys who had raced for the table at which they now sat drifted that way and one of the women waved them over. The barrel racers made room and soon everyone was seated at the small table. The guy who had winked at Kait earlier met Em's gaze across the room and lifted his glass. She wasn't certain what his message was, but she returned the salute. He was cute and she was feeling like she wanted to cut loose a little.

It was good to be out. Good not to be mulling over the situation with Selma. Or Darion. Or Jess.

If beer and cute cowboys couldn't cure her of worrying, then she was in more trouble than she knew.

"Earth to Em..."

She jerked her attention to Mallory. "Sorry. Where were we?"

"Apparently *we* were studying the cowboys across the room."

Em gave her friend a you-caught-me smile as she realized that she'd stared at the guy for just a little too long.

Mallory rolled her eyes. "I can't believe you."

"How so?"

"Traveling with a Hayward, yet ogling some guy across the room."

Emma gave a casual shrug. "The guy across the room never tried to kill my fun."

"What do you mean?" Mallory frowned as she spoke, so Em leaned her forearms on the table and prepared to fill in the blanks.

"Jess was like a second brother. I couldn't get away with anything when he was around."

"Is he still killing your fun?"

"Believe it or not, he still treats me like he did when I was in high school." Or he had when they'd first started driving. Now…not so much. Which was another reason to be ogling the guy across the room.

"Convince him you're not in high school."

"I think we'll continue as we are."

Mallory gave Em a sad shake of her head. "Hopeless."

"What can I say? Some things are just not meant to be." Before she finished speaking, someone put a hand on Kait's chair, pulling it out. Em turned, ready to defend the chair, and found herself staring into Wes Fremont's warm brown eyes. He smiled that cocky smile of his, making his cheeks crease. "Emma Sullivan. It's been a while."

She gave a small laugh, more at Mallory's comical expression, which clearly said, "How are you attracting all these hot guys?" than at Wes.

"Yes," she agreed. "It has."

"I'm thinking…two years?"

"Almost." She and Wes had traveled the college circuit together before she quit. They'd never talked a lot, but she'd noticed him. It was hard not to, since he'd been one of the best-looking guys in college rodeo. Time had been kind to him—if anything, he looked even better.

"Mind if I sit for a bit?"

Em looked at Mallory, who said, "Just don't let anyone get that other chair or Kait will have a conniption."

"We wouldn't want that," Wes said as he pulled his chair a little closer to Em than was necessary and sat, putting his beer on the table. "Can I get you guys something?"

"Kait's handling it."

"Ah." He glanced back at Em. "Not competing anymore?"

"Sold my horse."

"There are other horses out there."

"Let me rephrase that. I can't afford a good barrel horse, so no, I'm not competing."

"Have you looked into sponsors?" She frowned at him and he shrugged before saying in a low voice, "You were good."

He spoke in a way that felt distinctly intimate. Strange to think that he'd been watching her back in the day. She'd had no idea.

Kait came back with two pitchers, saying that she

didn't want to wait in that mob again, and settled in her chair. "Huh. Imagine that. My chair is still here."

"I sense a story," Wes said, but Kait simply waved her hand.

"I'll be back with the glasses in a sec."

"I'll help."

"I can handle it." Kait pushed her way through the people and came back a short time later with five glasses. "One for good measure," she said.

Wes did the honors and the four of them talked rodeo as the crowd in the bar began to swell, and it wasn't all competitors. Some of the out-of-town rodeo fans had discovered the place, too, probably due to the wonder of social media. She scanned the bar to see if Dermott had caught up with Chase, her heart doing a quick double beat when she realized that standing next to Chase was her very own travel partner.

Jess was there, looking better than any guy in the room, including the one sitting next to her, who apparently thought he was a gift to the world.

Jess, who'd sworn he was going to have an early night.

He turned, as if sensing her scrutiny, dark eyes zeroing in on her, making her feel very much as she had the last time he and Len had found her at a party when she'd been underage.

Emma pulled her gaze back to her beer without acknowledging him. So he'd changed his mind and come out to the bar. Big deal. She was still going to make a night of it.

"Are you all right?"

She jerked as Wes touched her leg beneath the table. He'd been inching closer, but this was too close. She moved her thigh a few inches, dislodging his hand. He gave her a knowing smile, although she had no clue as to what he thought he knew.

When she chanced another glance at Jess, he was once again in conversation with Chase, yet she had a hard time bringing her attention back to Wes, who'd just cleared his throat. A very crowded bar and the only guy she was now aware of was Jess. The cute cowboy sitting with Lara's group paled by comparison.

Had he come to keep an eye on her? Watch her back?

She knew he wouldn't be thrilled about her heading out alone with the rodeo crowd. She saw his point, but didn't know how she felt about him doing the watchdog thing—*if* that was what he was doing. Flattered in one sense. Frustrated in another. And, just to keep the alliteration going, fearful about where this thing between them might be heading. Flattered, frustrated, fearful. A mix of emotions not at all conducive to the grand evening she had planned for herself.

Wes was so close now that she could feel the heat from his body. She did her best to focus on Mallory and Kait and their stories of trying to live together, work full-time jobs and maintain their small farm, until Wes pressed his thigh against hers under the guise of having to move closer as the table behind them became more crowded. Emma couldn't edge away, so she gave him a dark look instead. He smiled at her.

She smiled back—a deadly smile. He was going down in flames, yet he didn't seem to realize that his mission had failed. If he continued to press in on her, she was going to have to resort to stomping his instep, but rather than cause a ruckus at the table, she slid her chair back as far as she was able—which wasn't far.

"I need to visit the ladies'," she murmured as she struggled to her feet, no easy task when her thighs were still practically under the table, and squeezed behind his chair. A second later, she heard Wes get up and start to follow her. Somehow she managed not to stop abruptly, so that he ran into her, and continued on into the short hallway between the bar area and the billiards room where the restrooms were located. There she did stop, just in front of the door, and she turned to Wes.

He smiled down at her and had the audacity to prop his hand on the knotty pine wall just over her head.

"When I come back from the restroom, I want you gone."

His cocky smile wavered, but only for a second, and then it came back, full force. "You don't mean that."

All she had to do was to lift her knee. He was open and vulnerable and unaware of her intentions. A quick shot to the family jewels and he'd understand just how deeply she meant it. However...

She pulled in a breath. "I'm not in the market, Wes. Go find someone else."

"But—" he leaned closer, his breath fanning her face as he said "—I'm a guy who thrives on challenge."

That did it. But before Em could lift her knee, Wes suddenly stumbled sideways, barely catching his balance before Jess pushed him again, toward the billiard room.

"Jess!" Emma scrambled after them as Jess backed Wes into the smaller room. Wes's legs came up against a table as the stunned players fell back.

"Jess!"

He turned his head to look at her and Wes took a swing at him, hitting him in the side of the head with a resounding crack and as Jess reeled sideways—and that was when Emma saw that Wes was holding a cue ball in his hand. Jess didn't go down, but as he fought for balance, blood streaming down the side of his face from a cut above his eyebrow, Wes pulled back his arm to hit him again. That was when Emma yanked the pool cue away from the guy standing next to her and stepped forward, waving it at Wes.

"Stop!"

As Wes's attention shifted, Jess regained his balance and managed to clip Wes a good one in the chin, making him stagger back against the table. Emma turned and waved the cue at Jess. "You, too. Just…*stop*!"

"Cops are coming."

The casual announcement came from somewhere behind her and Emma rolled her eyes. Just what she needed. She waved the cue at Wes again, then at Jess. If she played favorites, then Jess would never hear the end of being rescued by a woman.

It would serve him right, but…she couldn't do it.

"You heard them," Em said. "Cops are coming, guys. Maybe you should get out of here."

Wes glared at her, then pushed his way through the crowd. Jess came up to her, seemingly unfazed by the fact that she'd saved him, but he didn't touch her. Before he could say anything, she handed the cue back to the stunned guy she'd taken it from and muttered, "I do not want to spend the night in jail."

He nodded and took her by the hand, leading her through the crowd and out the exit next to the men's room. As the door closed behind them, Emma heard a truck engine start. Puffs of exhaust came from the tailpipes of an oversize red Chevy.

Jess let out a breath and put a hand up to his dripping cut, then pulled it away and grimaced. "Am I still pretty?"

"Get in the truck."

His eyebrow—the good one—lifted.

"Go," Emma repeated, taking hold of his shoulder and pulling him toward the vehicle. Headlights were blasting toward them and she wanted to get out of there before the deputies arrived. When they reached the rig, she simply said, "Keys."

He tossed them to her and she opened the door, waited for him to get into the passenger seat and then started the engine. They pulled out of the driveway just as the sheriff's vehicle pulled in. Apparently a lumbering truck and camper didn't look like a getaway rig, because the deputies roared past them, coming to a stop in front of the bar, the wheels of the cruiser half on, half off the sidewalk.

Emma let out a sharp breath as she gripped the wheel tighter, keeping one eye on the rearview mirror all the way back to the rodeo grounds, fully expecting red-and-blue lights at any second. Beside her Jess sat silently putting pressure on his wound. They'd made a clean getaway.

But now they had to deal with the matters before them instead of calling it a night.

Emma was angry. Beyond angry.

She had reason. Wes had been…himself…and Jess had tailed her to the bar and caused a scene. But given the chance, he would do it all over again.

Still, now was not the time to defend himself. Not

when Emma wheeled the truck into the rodeo grounds so sharply that he was thrown sideways.

Yes. Definitely angry.

She parked in their spot, which was still open, turned off the engine and tossed him the keys before getting out of the rig. Jess sat holding the keys for a split second, then followed her out of the vehicle. She motioned toward the camper with her head, her mouth so tight that it was going white beneath her lip gloss. "Let's see if you need stitches."

He was fairly certain from the amount of blood pouring down his face, leaving a sticky trail down his neck and soaking his shirt, that he needed something. Emma got the hot water flowing in the tiny sink and pulled out a roll of paper towels that'd been stashed in the cupboard below.

"Do what you can," she ordered. "And get out of that shirt."

"Any particular order you want me to do those things?"

Her lips curled at him. Jess reached out and took the towels, unrolling a few and tearing them off, holding her gaze, doing his best to read her as he plastered the wad up against the side of his forehead. She rolled off more, dampened them and handed them to him.

"Can't do much until the blood stops," she said in a grim tone.

"You don't have to stay." She gave him a look that said, yeah, she did, and Jess closed his mouth. If he told her she was acting a lot like Selma, she'd probably clock his other temple.

Eventually the blood slowed and Jess used the small shaving mirror propped next to the kitchen sink to clean the cut, then wipe the blood off his neck and chest after undoing a few buttons on his shirt.

"Let me see it," Emma demanded, so he turned to her. She frowned as she studied the cut. "Do you have butterflies?"

"Am I a bull rider?"

She didn't respond, so he pulled the medical kit out of a drawer and handed it to her. She opened it while he once again put pressure on the cut. She found a butterfly closure and unpeeled the wrapper. Jess took the towel away from his face and she leaned closer, her lips forming a perfect pout as she concentrated on placing the butterfly just so, bringing the edges of the wound together.

"I'm lucky you're not squeamish," he said, more to distract himself from the way her scent enveloped him, making him want to reach for her, than because he actually felt lucky.

"I grew up with too many brothers to be squeamish."

He grimaced as she put pressure on the edges of the adhesive closure. "Done?"

"You should put that shirt in a bucket of cold water."

"As opposed to throwing it away?"

She gave a small shrug. "It could be saved, but it's up to you."

Fine. If the shirt could be saved, he'd save it. Emma's lips parted as he started unbuttoning it the rest of the way, as if she was going to tell him to stop. But she didn't. Her gaze held on his fingers as they worked the buttons out of the holes. And then she swallowed.

"Emma?"

Her eyebrows drew together, but she didn't look at his face, so he stopped with the buttons and lifted her chin with his fingers. Her gaze came up. Defiantly, as if willing him to believe that his being bare-chested had no effect on her. And then he felt her shiver.

It wasn't from the cold, since it was about eighty degrees in the small camper.

Em scowled at him. "I should have kicked Wes in the nuts. I almost did, you know."

Jess's mouth twitched as she grabbed the topic out of thin air. "Did you?"

She nodded. "He's a jerk."

"Glad you think so."

She swallowed again. "That doesn't mean I think you're much better."

"You think I'm a jerk?" he asked softly.

"I…" Her voice trailed and she exhaled, her breath feathering over his chest, making his groin tighten. When she met his eyes then, her gaze solemn, almost pained, he had no problem interpreting. She was teetering on a precipice. The same precipice he was on. He needed to step away, to bring them both back from the edge…but how was he supposed to do that when she stepped closer, running her hands from his shoulders to his biceps?

"Em…"

She let out a ragged breath, closed her eyes and dropped her forehead against his chest, her silky hair tumbling forward against his bare skin. A gesture of frustration. Surrender. She had no more idea how to handle this than he did.

He wrapped his arms around her, running his hands up and down her back in a soothing motion. He didn't try to kiss her. He simply held her, well aware that she was probably seconds away from bolting. And when she bolted, he'd let her go and thank his lucky stars that things ended as they had.

But she surprised him. Instead of bolting, she pulled back, frowning slightly as she studied his face. Looking for…something.

Permission?

Encouragement?

Then his breathing stilled as she framed his face, lifted her lips and brushed them over his. The kiss was butterfly soft, yet it sent an electric jolt through him.

Sanity time.

No matter what he wanted to do here, one of them had to keep a clear head. But he didn't move, and when Emma slid her hands up to the back of his neck, pressing herself closer, he met her lips, kissed her. No more tentative exploration. He asked. She gave. Willingly, a husky sigh escaping her lips as he pulled her against him so tightly that she would have no doubt as to the effect she had on him. It didn't put her off. If anything she melted into him even more. He wanted her in the worst way. His hands traveled up under her shirt, skimming over her rib cage, his thumbs grazing over her perfect breasts. Her nipples were straining against the thin fabric of her lacy bra, and it was all he could do not to lose himself in the process of making love to her.

She shivered again in his arms and he forced himself to pull back when all he wanted to do was to press on. Claim her. Make her his. "We should stop," he muttered. Before he couldn't stop.

"I know." She let her hands trail down his chest, making his abs contract. "I'm going home."

His chin lifted as he stared down at her, stunned by her abrupt announcement. "You are?"

"I have to."

"Why?"

"Why? Well, because of *this*, for one thing. And because I have unfinished business at home for another."

"And…?" He sensed there was more.

The muscles in her jaw tightened momentarily before she said, "And because I'm messing up your rides."

He narrowed his eyes at her. "I thought we'd already settled that."

"No."

He reached out and took her by the shoulders. "Em… I am responsible for my rides. If I can't ride with distractions in my life, then I have no business going pro." He gave her a long, hard look, then dropped his hands. Em shifted her weight and regarded the floor.

There was no argument for his statement. If he couldn't get his head together, he shouldn't be riding. But he was going to get his head together. End of story.

"Okay," she said, raising her gaze back to his. "But what about—" she made a quick back-and-forth gesture between the two of them "—this."

"This. Yeah." He leaned back against the sink and folded his arms over his bare chest. If his shirt hadn't been such a mess, he would have buttoned it. Put up the barrier that Em so obviously needed. "What do you suggest?"

Because he had no answers. None that she was ready to accept anyway.

Em rubbed the back of her neck, then took hold of the table behind her, gripping it on either side of her thighs.

"Are you ready to go home?" he asked quietly.

"No." She shook her hair back. "I'm not."

"What if we came up with some rules?"

She turned her head to give him a cautious sideways look. "What kind of rules?"

"Strict hands-off rules."

Her eyebrows lifted. "For real?"

He drew in a breath and let it out again. "Yeah. For real."

She started slowly nodding, then let go of the table and folded her arms over her chest, mirroring his stance. "So it'd be hands off. Not an I-won't-touch-you-unless-you-ask kind of thing?"

"Hands off."

"No exceptions."

He gave his head a solemn shake. "None."

She tilted her head slightly, her reddish hair falling over her shoulders. "Does a handshake count?"

"Not as long as it's only one." He held out his hand and then a memory flashed into his head and he closed his fingers into a fist. "You will not spit into your hand."

A grudging smile transformed her face as she, too, remembered the solemn pact they'd made when she was twelve—if she would let Jess and Len go camping without raising a ruckus, then they would take her to the fall carnival and pay for every ride—and sealed with a spitty handshake.

"No spit." She held out her hand and he opened his, taking her fingers and giving them a brief shake.

Letting go was one of the hardest things he'd done in years.

Chapter Ten

Emma adjusted the sunglasses on her nose and propped a knee against the dashboard as she settled lower in her seat. The highway was bumpy—too bumpy to allow her to knit—so she gave up and stared at the road. Two days and one rodeo after Wes had smacked Jess in the bar, and they'd fallen into a routine that, while not exactly comfortable, was doable, and it saved her from having to go home.

She liked being on the road, meeting up with friends she hadn't seen in ages at the rodeos, seeing the country. Since reality would soon rear its ugly head and she'd have to return home and start making a living, she was determined to enjoy her freedom for as long as she could—and for that reason she was grateful to Jess for coming up with the stringent rules.

And abiding by them.

He'd ridden once since they'd made their pact and had done better than before. Or course, after three bad rides in a row, even a semi-decent ride looked good. LeClair was well ahead of him in the standings, as was Benny Two Feathers, and Wes was rising in the ranks. Emma wasn't vengeful, but she had enjoyed watching

Wes take a hard spill into a steaming pile of bull dung after his last ride. Somehow, it seemed appropriate.

Jess left the freeway fifty miles from Oakdale and pulled into a truck stop. While he fueled up, Em went inside to see about buying some junk food. They stopped cooking together after the showdown in the camper, neither of them feeling ready to spend that much time in the small space where they'd kissed. Twice. The camper was dangerous territory when it came to controlling impulses.

Emma was surviving on energy bars, and concession stand and gas station food. She wasn't certain what Jess was doing, but she hoped he was getting enough protein. Bull riders needed protein so that their bodies recovered from the beatings they took, but she wasn't his mom or his significant other, so she didn't ask him about it. He was well able to take care of himself.

She passed Jess going into the convenience store as she was coming out, bag of fried chicken in hand. He passed the keys over to her, their gazes meeting briefly before he continued on his way. They did a lot of silent communicating, which was better than the verbal kind, which somehow tended to get out of hand. Silence worked. He could prep for his rides and she could pretend that she was good with the way things were—and that touching him, even in the brief seconds it took to get his keys, didn't affect her. She was simply skittish after they'd kissed…come close to making love. If she hadn't backed off, they would have ended up in his bunk, and she still wondered what that would have been like. What kind of lover was Jess?

If he made love like he kissed…well, it would be an awesome experience.

Not that she was going to find out.

After what had happened with Darion, she wouldn't risk losing someone else close to her. After people made love, things changed. Judging from her current situation, even when people didn't make love, things could change.

Em got into the truck, set her drink in the holder and put the bag of chicken next to the gearshift, then leaned her head against the window. As Jess had said, things were never going to be the same between them, and she regretted that. However, that didn't mean they couldn't be *close* to the same again. They just needed time.

Emma sighed. What they needed was time *and* distance, but since they'd agreed to keep on keeping on, distance would have to wait. She'd rather ride with Jess, feeling edgy and uncertain, than go home and do battle before she was ready.

Besides…she had a growing suspicion that if she and Jess parted ways now, before working things out, that was that. She may never spend significant time with him again. She wasn't ready to cut him out of her life, so she had to tread carefully.

The door opened and Emma gave Jess a pleasant, if somewhat distant, smile—the same smile she gave to patrons of the diner that she didn't know well. And that was a sad reality but part of the pact—an unspoken part.

"Ready to ride?"

"The big question is, are you?" The stock contractor for that night's rodeo was known for having some of the toughest bulls in the region.

"Yeah," he said simply. "I am."

It was good to hear him sound so confident. Doubts had to be plaguing him after his run of less than stellar rides. Emma pulled out her phone. "What's the name of your draw?"

"Pick Me Up."

She tapped the name into her phone and chose one of the many videos that popped up, watched it, then chose another.

"What do you think?"

"I think you'd better watch your face." The bull had a habit of rearing steeply.

"Noted. Ty had the crap smashed out of his face just before he moved onto Skye's ranch."

"I remember seeing him around town sporting an awesome black eye and stitches." Emma shifted in her seat. They were talking again, falling into old habits. She cleared her throat, then pointedly put down her phone and pulled her sunglasses off the top of her head, placing them back onto her nose. She sensed Jess studying her out of the corner of his eye, but pretended not to notice.

Fifty miles and they'd be there. Jess would ride, she would watch. They'd get back into the truck and do it again. She'd feel tense and bothered and do her best to knit and ignore him. She'd forbid herself to think about kissing him, about how his big, work-roughened hands would feel skimming over her bare skin. The frustration continued.

Why didn't she go home?

Because she wasn't ready, and the fact that she was here, battling her hormones, pretending not to be overwhelmingly attracted to the guy sitting two feet away from her spoke volumes as to how unready she was.

A sigh escaped her lips and she froze, hoping that Jess hadn't heard it. Of course, that was hoping for too much.

"You okay?"

"Thinking about Selma."

For a brief moment, she thought that had been answer enough and she could go on brooding about her life and fighting to keep from sighing aloud. But no.

"What is the deal there, Em?" He shot her a quick look. "Why is she so hot to get you married off?"

"We agreed that we were only going to talk about superficial stuff," she murmured.

"Was that what we agreed upon?"

She couldn't see his eyes behind his dark glasses, but she had a feeling that his expression wasn't as politely distant as his words.

"I thought so."

"Huh." He adjusted his grip on the steering wheel.

Don't. Just...don't.

Emma couldn't help herself. She took the bait. "We agreed that we wouldn't delve into personal matters."

"I thought that meant personal between you and me."

Red flags fluttered. "No."

"We're trying to be friends, right? Wasn't that the purpose of the rules?"

"Your point?" Emma muttered.

"Last I heard, friends talked and not only about superficial stuff. Or do you only want to be acquaintances? Because if so, I don't know if I can successfully turn back the clock."

"Maybe you could try, because I feel better when we keep things...less personal."

"Right." His mouth tightened. Em knew because she was watching him out of the corner of her eye.

It sucked that she honestly couldn't think of him the same as she had before. She'd lost Darion by letting things get romantic and it appeared that the same thing had happened with Jess—the one guy who understood so much about her life.

"Do you think about Len?" She asked the question softly, knowing that she was doing exactly what she'd just complained about—getting personal.

"Every day."

She gave a silent nod. Same with her. She missed her brother, and after living the life he'd lived, taking risks, riding broncs, it seemed so wrong that he'd been taken out by a stupid car wreck.

"It opened up a big hole in my life. Things will never be the same."

Amen to that. And maybe that was life—things changing. No matter how badly a person didn't want them to.

"Don't smack me for asking," Jess said, instantly putting Em on edge, "but did Len's death have something to do with you hooking up with Darion?"

"If you don't want to be smacked, don't ask personal questions."

"I'll risk the smack."

He wasn't going to give it up. Not easily anyway. "Of course it did."

She turned and looked out the side window at the passing scenery. In her defense, she did love the guy... just not in the way she'd convinced herself she did. She'd painted a happy mental picture of the two of them settling into a mellow life together—told herself that it was enough. That wild attractions burnt out. And she could still see benefits to that kind of a relationship she'd developed with Darion—but not enough to ultimately overcome the feeling that she needed more than mellow. Darion would have been a great father. A great partner—in the friend sense.

She needed more.

She glanced over at Jess and her heart did an odd flutter beat.

Oh, yeah—he could definitely offer *more*, but she didn't need to lose a friend in the process. Regardless of how things had changed, they would eventually drift back toward normal. Jess would find a girlfriend—not Lara—and she would be a little sad, but accept it as the way life was, and things would be good again.

"A penny for them," Jess said, breaking the stiff silence.

Emma snorted. "Don't tempt me. I'm low on funds."

"And not about to share."

"We made a pact." Which he seemed hell-bent on breaking.

"That we did." They approached a small town, a handful of buildings hugging the highway, and Jess slowed the truck as they passed through. "But we can still talk."

Emma frowned as he slowly turned her way, the intensity of his expression, even with the dark glasses on, making her breath catch a little. "Eyes on the road," she muttered.

"And if I don't?"

She hit her palm with her fist.

Jess smiled at her, the I-don't-want-to-be-amused-but-I-am smile she hadn't seen since they'd stirred up all this trouble between them. Emma did her best not to react, but failed. Her insides tumbled. She needed a distraction. The truth would do.

"Darion helped me through rough times after Len passed." She bit the inside of her cheek as she thought back to first the numbness, then the tear-choked days that followed the funeral and finally the process of slowly putting her life back together with one vital piece missing. Her former study partner, Darion, had been there through all of it. She, who hated to depend on anyone, thanks to Selma's strict stand-on-your-own-two-feet—unless she was involved—upbringing, had come to depend on her friend. They'd grown closer. So close that she mistook her feelings for love—the romantic kind, not the friend kind. He'd made the same mistake and they'd come to their senses together, which had been a blessing.

And then he disappeared from her life. Not a blessing. Instead it left yet another hole that she was fighting to fill.

She was not going to fill it with Jess. Wasn't going to risk it.

They had three more weeks on the road. Then she would go home and he would continue to the last rodeos before the finals alone. Three weeks to hold strong, and to build another kind of strength—the Selma-resisting kind—before going home and taking control of her life.

Jess reached out to lightly touch her knee, instantly getting her attention. "Yeah. I know. No touching. That was supposed to be reassuring and brotherly."

Maybe that had been the intent but it felt like being touched by a guy she wanted to have touch her. Thankfully, he didn't seem to notice when she swallowed drily.

"We'll get through this, Em. I'll get my mojo back and we'll end the trip on a high note."

"You think?"

"Going to do my best to see that it happens that way."

She directed her attention forward again, watching the white lines disappear in front of the truck. "Yeah. Me, too."

JESS'S RIDE THAT night was better, but he couldn't say that he had his mojo back. Not when he came in third and was beat by Wes yet again. Wes, who never came close to keeping up with him in previous years.

Wes, whom he'd still like to stomp into the ground, more because of Emma than because of the cheap shot with the cue ball...although he could do some stomping on those grounds alone.

His plan of testing the waters before going pro was not working out the way he'd anticipated—on many levels.

He caught sight of Em making her way toward the truck ahead of him as the crowd left the stands and cars began pulling out of the parking lot. They were driving that night, heading across the state yet again for a rodeo that started at noon the next day. His event was last, but he wanted to get there in time to warm up. Not that he hadn't ever stepped out of a truck and headed straight to the alley minutes before he was on deck, but that wasn't his preferred method of operation.

When he caught up with Emma, she gave him a commiserating smile. She knew that even though he'd made the buzzer, he wasn't happy about it. "Next time," she said, giving him a sisterly clap on the upper arm. Every now and again she did that, probably in her quest to convince herself that if they treated each other like friends, that's all they would be. It wasn't working for him, and he'd wager it wasn't working that well for her either. She was jumpy around him in a way she'd never been before—as if she didn't trust him. Or herself.

She had cause.

"Yeah." He unbuckled the belt of his chaps, tossed them, along with his rope, vest and helmet, into the camper and locked the door. Em was already in the driver's seat, ready to start the engine. She often drove after he rode, but tonight he would have preferred to do it rather than focus on the disturbing trend of mediocrity in his rides.

But he put aside those wishes and instead got into the passenger seat, getting as comfortable as he could propped in the corner, his head against the window, arms crossed over his middle.

"Stop at Whitehall?" Several hundred miles away.

"If you have it in you."

She adjusted the side mirror instead of answering, then pulled out of their space and joined the line of trucks leaving the field. As soon as she was on the highway, Jess closed his eyes, thinking about plans gone wrong.

They weren't wrong. They just weren't working out on schedule. He had to believe that after quitting his job and making the plunge. The irony was that in years past, he'd been a force to be reckoned with, but now, after deciding to go for the prize, he wasn't riding as well as before.

Age? Or nerves?

Circumstances.

Tyler was ten minutes younger than him and doing spectacularly in the pros. Nerves? The only thing that made him nervous was not being financially stable. Em? She made him feel edgy, but not nervous.

Edgy, distracted, frustrated…afraid.

What was he afraid of?

Maybe he was afraid of screwing things up, making it a certainty that he never saw her again. More than that, he wanted her to feel relaxed around him. To know that she could count on him. That he was there for her if she needed him.

It didn't help that he wanted all of those of things, and he also wanted her in his bed.

He snorted at the thought and then raised an eyelid to see Em shifting her attention back to the road. "Funny dream," he murmured, closing his eye again.

"Already?"

"I'm a fast dreamer." He shifted in his seat, folded his arms a little more tightly over his chest. His shoulders were sore and one of his elbows had recently been hyperextended, but all in all, he was feeling pretty good—probably because his rides hadn't been good.

But this was his last bad ride—make that mediocre ride. From here on out it was championship material. And if not…then maybe he had to consider hanging up his dream. Working in construction for the rest of his life.

The thought didn't sit well. Now that he'd committed to his plan, he intended to see it out, even if it meant facing the fact that he was too old to do what he'd put off for too long.

JESS FELL ASLEEP for real about twenty minutes into the drive and Emma allowed herself the luxury of the occasional glance his way. He looked so good when he slept—not that he ever looked bad—she felt the need to indulge herself and admire him when he wasn't aware.

The trouble was, he usually was aware. His peripheral vision rivaled hers and more than once he'd caught her midstare. Her cheeks grew warm as she thought about it. A couple of months ago, it would have meant nothing to have been caught studying Jess. If he'd called her on it, she would have been able to articulate a reason for staring. His hair seemed different. He had a spot on his shirt. Stuff like that. But now, even if that was the reason she was staring, she felt shifty getting caught.

Because she was too darned aware of him as a man now. To make matters worse, every now and again, she caught him looking at her before she'd look away, pretend not to notice.

He was following their pact—for the most part—but he wasn't totally on board. If she made a move toward him, he would reciprocate. She knew it as certainly as she knew that her middle name was Rose. She was making things hard on him by staying, but he'd encouraged her to do so. Because he was a good guy? Or because…

She slammed her thoughts into a different direction. She didn't want to think that he was patiently waiting her out. Waiting for her hormones to get the best of her common sense and desire to keep him as a friend.

Was it selfish of her to stay on the road with him?

As near as she could tell, she wasn't doing him any favors by being there. His rides were not up to par. It might all be a coincidence. Bad rides happened—she knew that from her days on the circuit—but for a guy like Jess, a seasoned bull rider whom many said was more talented than his very talented twin, to have one bad ride after another…it had to be more than coincidence.

He stirred in his sleep and Em kept her eyes on the road, just in case. In a matter of weeks she'd be home, doing battle with Selma. That was what she needed to focus on. That and perhaps getting a better paying job and a roommate so that she was totally free of the family ranch.

In the old days, she might have asked to move in with Jess. As a friend. For a while. Now that was nigh unto impossible.

As he said, things had changed.

Emma pushed her hair back with one hand. She didn't dare turn on the radio, but for once, she didn't need the sound to keep her focused. Having Jess sleeping next to her kept her suitably on edge. The two hundred miles to Whitehall passed more quickly than she'd anticipated, so after a quick look at Jess, she'd pressed on.

Looking at him had been a mistake, because now she wanted to look again.

Emma adjusted her grip on the steering wheel as she peered at the road. There was always the possibility of a deer deciding to bound across the road, and she needed to be alert, not sidetracked by quick glances at her seatmate.

A hundred miles passed and she began to think she was going to make it all the way to the Sulfur Mountain rodeo grounds, but a sudden yawn convinced her otherwise. She rolled through a tiny town and started looking for a side road to pull off on before serious fatigue set in, when she saw the campground sign. Perfect.

She'd gotten them most of the way there and had worked out a few things in her head. The one question she hadn't answered was the one about whether she was being selfish by staying with him.

Chapter Eleven

The truck bounced, waking Jess. No, he wasn't being slammed into the dirt by a raging bovine. He was in a truck, his body stiff from sleeping upright after a mediocre ride.

"Sorry," Emma said. "That pothole came out of nowhere."

"No biggie." He grimaced as he shifted his body.

"We're at a campground." Emma pulled up in front of the office and when she reached for the door handle, he said, "I'll go." He needed to move.

He stepped out of the truck into the crisp night air without his sleep-numbed leg collapsing, although he had to limp a few steps before the blood started flowing again. By the time he got to the dark office, he was walking normally. Sort of.

He had no idea where they were, but the place smelled of damp grass and evergreens. He guessed they were somewhere near Whitehall, their destination, but he couldn't pinpoint the locale. Hopefully, if they weren't in Whitehall, they were close enough to make an easy morning drive to the rodeo grounds in Sulfur.

There was a sign on the office door, outlining rules and regulations, but no one inside, so Jess went back to the truck. Emma rolled down the window as he approached. "They check the sites in the morning. We pay then."

"Great. There's a couple of spots up there." She pointed straight ahead to two empty sites just visible in the headlights.

"Go ahead and park. I'll walk."

When Emma turned off the engine after parking, the night seemed abnormally silent, and Jess's boots in the gravel sounded abnormally loud. The other campsites were dark and even the highway was quiet, making Jess wonder what time it was.

Emma got out of the truck as he pulled his phone out of his shirt pocket, rolling her shoulders and her neck before heading back to the camper. He turned on the phone, glanced at the time.

Three a.m.?

Where were they? They should have reached Whitehall by midnight.

A semitruck rolled by on the highway, breaking the silence as Jess reached the camper. Emma was inside and he waited until she emerged, a sleeping bag in one hand, her small gym bag in the other. Jess hoped that it didn't start raining during their travels. Then they'd be stuck together in the small space of the camper.

"Where are we?"

"About thirty miles from the rodeo grounds." She stifled a yawn as she spoke. "I didn't have another thirty miles in me."

"Aren't we supposed to be just shy of two hundred miles away from the campsite?"

"Yeah. Well, I was buzzed until about half an hour

ago, so I pushed on. This way we can sleep in and still get there in plenty of time."

He wouldn't need to sleep late, since he'd been out for most of the drive, but Emma would. Faint shadows showed under her eyes and her face seemed paler than usual. She was exhausted. "You want to take the camper tonight?"

She gave him a startled look. "Why?"

"Because I slept for six hours and you didn't."

"No." She pushed past him and headed toward the truck.

"Em, you drove all night."

"I said, no," she called over her shoulder in a harsh whisper, reminding him that people were sleeping nearby. Jess followed her and opened the truck door while she juggled her load, trying to free a hand.

"Thank you." She closed her mouth and tilted her chin, obviously waiting for him to leave before making her nest in the back seat.

"Last chance."

"Thank you, no. I don't want to be responsible for you not being in tip-top shape tomorrow."

Jess let out a snort. "I ride bulls. I'm never in tip-top shape."

"Whatever," she muttered as she dumped the stuff she carried onto the seat. She started unrolling the bag and Jess backed off. He'd tried. If she preferred to sleep in the truck, so be it.

He made his way to the privies, noted that the path was well lit and there was no one lurking about. Emma would be fine. As soon as he was back in the camper, he started shucking out of his clothes, tossing them onto the bench. He'd showered before they'd started driving, so he intended to climb back into them when he got out of bed.

He was halfway out of his pants when a shriek ripped through the night. Tripping and stumbling, he dragged the jeans back up as he headed for the door, heart hammering, ready to do battle. He thrust it open and tripped over one of his boots, barely keeping his footing as he plunged out the door to find Emma a few yards away from the camper, waving her arms and swatting the air around her head.

"Em!"

As soon as she heard his voice, saw the open door behind him, she headed for it, still swatting wildly. But instead of climbing inside to safety, she took refuge between him and the camper, ducking low.

"Bats," she said, her voice squeaky. "Lots of them. They dive bombed me when I stepped out of the Sani-Hut."

Relief ripped through him, followed by the urge to laugh. Reaction. It wasn't because she'd looked funny swatting and running in circles…even though she had.

"I thought I was going to have to fight off a bear or something."

Emma cautiously scanned the night sky for winged marauders. "I'm never going to sleep now."

Jess stepped back, determined not to follow instinct and pull her closer, give her a reassuring hug. She didn't need to be touched, and he didn't need to be touching.

She brushed her hair back. "I must have looked ridiculous."

"Well…" Jess said slowly. "You didn't look dignified."

She blew out a breath, rubbing her hands over her

upper arms and making no move to leave the space between Jess and camper.

He shifted his weight, folding his arms over his bare chest. "Want me to walk you to the door?" Which was about eight feet away.

"I can make it." Emma craned her neck to peer past him into the darkness.

"Maybe I could go halfway with you." Like four feet.

She scowled at him. "Not funny. You have no idea what it feels like to have those things buzz you."

"Pretty creepy?"

"The worst." She suppressed a shiver. "I'm going now."

Jess nodded. She hesitated, then squared her shoulders and marched around the side of the camper.

"Shout out when you get there," Jess called after her.

"Oh, shut up." The door opened and closed and once Emma was safe, Jess looked over his shoulder at the place where the bats had buzzed her, before climbing back into the camper, smiling a little. He didn't think Emma being frightened after driving forever was funny…but it was good to see her acting like her old self. Because then he could act like his old self and that would help him get through this road trip with his sanity intact.

BATS WERE DEFINITELY off her favorite animal list.

Even nestled deep in her sleeping bag, Emma could feel the odd sensation of having small winged bodies swoop around her, brushing her with their wings—or maybe they'd been so close it had only felt as if they'd been touching her. They had meant her no harm, but in her sleep-deprived state, she'd been in no condition to deal with unusual circumstances, such as a bat attack or Jess offering her the camper.

What was that about?

It was a nice gesture, but she wasn't going to encourage nice gestures. Not that particular gesture anyway. Like it would do her any good to sleep in his bed. To bury her nose in his sheets and smell his scent. Emma closed her eyes. No—that wouldn't do at all. She needed to stay strong in order to stay on the road and get their relationship back on track.

The bat incident had helped. For a few minutes it felt like old times.

She adjusted her position, tucking her hands up close to her chin as she felt her body begin to relax.

Maybe bats weren't so bad, after all.

The next morning, she woke when the campground manager came around collecting the space rent. She lay still, listening to Jess discuss the upcoming rodeo with the man, who was apparently a fan, then reached down on the floorboards to retrieve her phone.

Ten o'clock!

She sat straight up, clutching the bag to her chest and looking around wildly. The sun shone brightly, birds sang. She could hear people talking in the distance and the sound of chopping wood. A woman strolled by with her small fluffy dog, nodding politely at her. Emma nodded back and then lay down again.

How could it be ten o'clock? She'd said she wanted to sleep in, but this was ridiculous. She shimmied into her clothing, tugging and pulling while keeping low enough in the seat to stay out of sight—no easy trick, and another reason she preferred to rise early—and then opened the truck door.

Jess was nowhere to be seen, so she made the trip to the bathroom without being attacked by bats. The camper door was open as she trekked back, which she assumed was an invitation to stop by.

At that point, she'd kill for a shower.

Or coffee—which she could smell.

Long, long night.

Jess came out of the camper as she approached, a cup of coffee in each hand.

"You are my hero," she said as she took the cup.

"Everybody says that."

She smirked at him and took a drink, savoring the taste of the warm, dark brew. Jess made a decent cup of coffee. "We should get going soon."

"No hurry."

"Maybe I can grab a shower, then?"

"I saved water for you."

"I'm not going to repeat my hero comment."

"Suit yourself." He smiled at her, then shifted his gaze to the mountains on the opposite side of the highway. Things felt…better. More normal.

Closer to the way they used to be. Progress.

And all it had taken were a few bats.

Jess won by default at Sulfur Mountain.

His ride had been a tick above adequate, but since he'd been the only guy to ride to the buzzer, his score of seventy-seven got him a win. And a check. And a feeling of renewed determination.

Not because of the win, but because of a clarifying moment he'd had as he left the arena.

In past seasons, he'd focused only on the ride ahead of him, not on the season's outcome, because, due to his job, he might not make enough rides to qualify for finals. Now he needed finals and he was concentrating on the big picture and worrying about what happened if his plan didn't work. What then? What kind of job he could get and where. What his future would be.

No one could tell the future, and he was wasting his time trying.

He needed to channel his twin, just as he'd done when his safety net was still there, and not worry about the outcomes of rodeos weeks away. He needed to make each rodeo the most important aspect of his journey, instead of wrapping himself in a vicious cycle of what-if thoughts.

His long-term goals were different, but his short-term goals were exactly the same.

Emma got into the driver's seat. Her aviators hid her eyes from him, but he figured that if he could see her eyes, he would read mild disapproval.

"Go ahead," he said.

"Go ahead and what?" She sounded perplexed. "Drive?"

"Give me a critique of my ride."

"Ah." She started the truck and, after checking the mirrors, pulled onto the road leading out of the rodeo grounds. She waited until they were out on the highway proper before saying, "Your ride was fine. You stayed on."

"I was close to coming off." Due to anticipating a spin that never happened. He'd recovered, but he shouldn't have.

"Yeah. You were." He watched as her forehead furrowed above the sunglasses. "It's like…you're psyching yourself out."

"Exactly," he murmured, propping his sore knee on the dash.

"You're aware, then."

"Yeah."

"Hmph." The soft grunt was her only reply as she maneuvered into the passing lane to get around a very slow truck.

He kept his eyes on her profile, watched the corner of her mouth move as she worked things over. Finally, when he was about to ask what was going on in her head, she said, "I distract you."

"What's new?"

"Okay…maybe it's more than that. Maybe I jinx you."

He gave a sputtering laugh. "What? I don't believe in jinxes."

She gave him a look over the top of her glasses before bringing her gaze back to the road. "But you do believe in distractions."

"I've been distracting *myself.* Looking at things wrong."

She was silent for a few seconds, then said, "Things are going to change now?"

"Yeah. I'm going to ride like I used to. As if there was no tomorrow, because in seasons past, when I was winning, I didn't care about tomorrow."

"I don't know, Jess. Not caring about tomorrow sounds more like Tyler than you."

"Yes. It does. My point is that as a pro bull rider, I need a plan, but I can't let the plan ruin my rides."

"I guess." She shot him another dubious look, giving him the feeling that she thought he was trying to talk his way around the truth.

"It's not you, Em. Okay? I like having a driver along."

And I like being around you, even if you do drive me a little crazy.

That part remained unsaid for obvious reasons.

"No more talk about distractions and jinxes." When Emma didn't answer immediately, he added, "Agreed?"

Emma let out a small breath. "Agreed."

EMMA KEPT HER eyes on the road. She was glad that Jess was coming to a place in his head where he felt comfortable and confident. Half of any battle, even one with a bull, was the mental game, and Jess's had been off for a while now.

She still didn't buy his assertion that she was not at least partially to blame. He'd won a lot when she wasn't around. Now…not so much. But if that was the position he took, she wasn't going to fight him.

"Hey." She looked over at him, wondering why he was still awake when he usually conked out shortly after they started driving. "We have an extra two days, you know."

Please don't ask to go back to Gavin.

"Yeah?" She slowed as she approached two trucks driving side by side, the one in the passing lane inching slowly by the other. At this rate, they'd be behind these two big boys for miles and miles.

"Here's my plan. We stop in Butte and do laundry."

"So far, so good."

"Drive back to Whitehall and camp there."

"Okay."

"Then…" He sounded as if he were waiting for a drum roll. "We go to the caverns."

Emma grimaced. "Like caves?"

"No, The Caverns strip club. You'll love it."

"I'm going to hurt you."

He laughed. "Yes. Caves. Lewis and Clark Caverns. I've always wanted to go."

"Why?" One corner of her mouth tightened. Why would anyone want to go to a cave?

"Come on, Em. Do the tourist thing with me."

"I'll do the laundry thing with you and think about it."

"Cool." He shifted his position, folding his arms over his chest and dropping his chin to his chest.

"Uh...so we're only going as far as Butte tonight?"

"Yeah. Butte. Breakfast. Laundry."

"All right." Then they'd discuss the crazy cave idea. If she worked things right, she'd help him see the sense of driving on across the state and having some downtime there before his next rodeo.

Chapter Twelve

"I'll pay your admission," Jess said as they waited for their turn to join a group on a cavern tour.

"Darned right, you will." Emma tipped up her chin and narrowed her eyes at him. "And remember your promises."

They'd discussed the matter at length and Emma had made it clear that she wasn't claustrophobic or afraid of the dark. But she'd never been in a cave and wasn't certain she liked the idea. Jess had taken care not to press her. In fact, he'd let the matter drop and then, out of the blue, Em had agreed.

"If I embarrass myself by freaking out, you'll be there."

Promise number one. "I will."

"And if I start pushing my way through the crowd to get out, you'd better be my blocker."

A slightly different take on promise number two, which had been to get her back to the surface as quickly and quietly as possible. "Will do."

Jess paid and they joined their group and their teenage tour guide. The two-mile hike from the lodge to the cave entrance seemed to go a long way toward calming Em's nerves, and when it was time for their small group to descend into the caverns, she seemed perfectly at ease. Right up until the tour guide made them promise not to disturb the bats.

She gave him an accusatory look. "You did this on purpose."

Jess reached out to take her hand. "I did not."

She squeezed his fingers, then slipped her hand free, but the feeling of easy camaraderie remained. They made their way down ridiculously steep stairs into a world of stalagmites and stalactites, darkness and dampness. And Jess felt his breathing start to go shallow.

Oh, no. Was *he* claustrophobic?

Maybe it was the narrow staircase that seemed to hang out over dark nothingness that made him uneasy. Meanwhile, Em moved smoothly down the stairs, craning her neck to see what was ahead of them. Once they hit solid ground, the guide started to speak and Jess tried to focus, but found that instead he was wondering how much all the rock above them weighed. And what happened if the earth decided to shift?

He started sweating, despite the cool temperature.

"Look at that, Jess!" Emma pointed out a beautifully colored stalagmite. Or was it a stalactite? He was too focused on survival to ask.

"Wow."

She turned a frowning look his way. "Are you okay?"

"Yeah. Totally."

One eyebrow arched up, and then she turned to follow the group. Jess walked immediately behind her, doing his best not to think about tons of earth. They were in a huge space that people had visited for over a century. The walls and formations were awe-inspiring. And so was the thought of hitting daylight.

"Are you all right?" Em asked a few minutes later.

"No." He didn't even try to lie. "I'm not a cave person."

Em turned toward him, and even in the dim light, he could read more concern than amusement in her expression. "Really?"

"Really." He felt better because of the confession. "How long until we get out of this hellhole?"

"Shouldn't be too much longer."

"Please don't lag too far behind," the guide called.

"Oh, don't worry about me lagging," Jess muttered as they caught up with the group, which was stopped at a formation illuminated by rainbow lighting. Emma leaned her shoulder into his as the guide droned on and Jess closed his eyes. Focused on breathing and the firm warmth of Emma's shoulder.

"I'm right here," she murmured when they had to squeeze between two pillars before emerging into a larger room.

Jess didn't say anything, but he appreciated the fact that she *was* there, giving him something to focus on besides dying.

The tour continued, and when they eventually hit the sunlight, about five days later, Jess let out a relieved breath. "Finally."

Emma bit her lip as the people in their group moved around them. Didn't come close to laughing, even though he could now read nothing but amusement in her expression, and he appreciated that. "Maybe I can plan the outings in the future."

"Yeah." Although there wouldn't be any outings for the remainder of the tour. The schedule was tight. "And right now, I'd like to get in the truck and drive." His spelunking days were over.

They walked back to the parking area, both lost in their thoughts, Jess dealing with the fact that he'd just discovered a previously unknown phobia and Em…? Who knew? He'd just given her a lot of ammo and she'd chosen to do nothing with it. Yet.

"Hey," he said as she unlocked the truck door. As she glanced back at him, the wind caught her hair and she caught it on one side of her face. "I…uh…appreciate you not laughing at me."

"I'm laughing on the inside."

But she wasn't. He was certain of that. "Although—" he said slowly, rubbing a hand over the back of his neck "—it might have been better if you did."

She didn't pretend not to understand his meaning. Not that long ago, before this crazy attraction had taken hold, she would have laughed her butt off.

"I'll work on that. But…" She started to smile, worked to keep her lips from curving. Lost the battle. "You should have seen yourself. All wild-eyed and… I don't know…" She bit her lip. "I would have blocked for you."

"If I'd been sure of the way out, I would have let you. I had no idea I was claustrophobic." He kicked the toe of his boot into the dirt. Smiled a little as he met her eyes, then his expression sobered. "Kind of makes me wonder what other issues I have that I don't know about." Obviously bulls weren't a problem, but what about surviving a future that didn't involve a safety net? He thought he was okay with that, but he'd thought he'd be okay with caves, too.

"Whatever they are, you'll deal."

"You know that I don't like surprises."

"You don't like them, but you can handle them. You handled the cave. You can handle taking the plunge into pro bull riding."

His eyes narrowed. "How'd you know what I was thinking?"

"How could I not know?" Emma spoke on a note of amused weariness, a faint smile playing on her sexy mouth, then she leaned back against the truck and looked at him in a way that made him feel like he was the younger of the two. "You and I…" She dropped her gaze as her voice trailed off. Cleared her throat.

For one charged moment, he thought she was going to say something unexpected—something he was pretty sure he wanted to hear—but instead she looked toward the road. "We'd better get going."

"Yeah." The atmosphere had changed and now Emma was all business when he was still thinking about taking her by the wrist and pulling her a little closer, leaning in and kissing her. As a thank-you, of course. Nothing else.

Right…and he'd be signing up for the next cave tour just as soon as he possibly could.

JESS HAYWARD COULD face a raging bull without blinking, but being in a cave had seized him up.

Unexpected.

Equally unexpected was the fact that, other than the potential for bat attack, Emma loved every minute of the tour. And the bats had been kind of cute all huddled up on the walls and ceilings of the cave. As the tour went deeper into the cavern system, there'd been no bats at all. Just one freaked-out bull rider trying to hold it together until he saw sunlight.

Emma didn't want to be touched by the fact that Jess was not only weirded out by being underground—he'd been up-front about it. A guy who'd ridden bulls with broken bones, who didn't blink when he drew the roughest man killer on the circuit, who had raced out of his camper, tripping over his pants, thinking he might have to fight a bear instead of bats, had confessed his fears the second time she'd asked. Remarkable for a chin-up, hide-the-pain kind of guy.

Emma was impressed.

As a friend.

She needed to keep that small fact front and center. They were friends. Nothing more.

When he'd asked her earlier how she'd known what he'd been thinking, she'd almost told him that she felt closer to him than to any guy on earth. True or not, that would have been a mistake. They were walking a thin line and she had to do her best to stay on it.

She turned on music and they traveled without talking. Jess watched bull riding videos on his phone, and Emma debated what her life would be like when she returned home. There would, of course, be a showdown with Selma, and she was going to have to stand up to her stepmom—explain that she was going to live her life her way. Selma wouldn't listen, Emma would have to explain again...

Maybe if her father had stood up to Selma a time or two over the years things would be different, but her dad was the retiring sort. He didn't like confrontation and was appreciative of his wife, who met the world head-on, so he didn't have to.

Her dad was her dad. A gentle soul who only wanted to ranch and tinker in his shop. Selma was as protective of him as she was of her children. It was an odd relationship that worked amazingly well, and since it worked well for him, it seemed that Emma's dad believed it worked equally well for his kids.

"You want to catch a meal tonight?"

Jess's sudden question brought her back to the present and Emma shook her head without looking at him. "Concession stand burger will work for me."

"Probably won't be anything open until tomorrow."

"I'll hit my junk food stash."

"I'll buy."

She looked at him then. "It's not the money."

"Then what?"

"I...just want a night to myself." She did. Things were going well between them right now—why chance having another upset before his next ride?

He narrowed his eyes at her before saying, "All right."

He shifted his gaze forward and Emma did the same. It was best for both of them if he focused on his ride instead of going out with her—even for a quick dinner. Things had a strange way of turning around on them and she wanted him to be 100 percent into his game.

"You know that you're not distracting me." Jess was no longer watching the road. A quick sideways glance met his gaze.

She brought her eyes forward again. "That's what you told me."

"And that's what you need to believe. Dinner with me isn't going to hurt anything."

Emma's mouth opened to ask him how he knew what she was thinking, but caught herself and closed it again. "Agreed. But I still want a night to myself."

"Consider it done." He spoke flatly, telling her that he didn't believe her, but he wasn't going to push. Much. "You should eat better."

Torn between exasperation and irritation, Emma gave him a deadly look. He held up his hands in a gesture of surrender and she gritted her teeth together as she pulled into the rodeo grounds.

Now she felt even better about spending the night alone.

JETSAM WAS A brindle half-Brahman bull with turned-down horns and a look of malice in his eye. As he was squeezed into the chute, he kicked sideways a couple of times, making the rails ring. Jess gave the animal a once-over, then climbed up on the rail and started working his rope onto him. Jetsam gave him a long baleful look and tossed his head as Jess balanced over him, a foot on each rail and slid down into place, his spotter keeping a hand on his vest in case Jetsam took exception to having a rider on his back. Chase pulled the rope, allowing Jess to adjust his grip.

For the first time in weeks, he felt the calm. Felt himself slide into the moment, blocking out everything except for the bull sweating and twitching beneath him. The gate swung open and Jetsam slammed into action. Jess was with him and stayed with him, countering the bull's every move, staying deep and square, absorbing the shock of the pounding spins and kicks through his feet. When the buzzer sounded, Jess looked over his free arm and started to swing his leg over the bull's head when the animal twisted and reared, snagging Jess's leg just as he released his grip. Jetsam gave a mighty toss of his head and Jess flopped through the air, landing hard on his side before the bull butted him, rolling him into the dirt.

The next thing he was cognizant of were hands under his arms, lifting him as he staggered first to a knee and then to his feet. As his head cleared, he caught sight of Jetsam trotting out of the arena, tail high, none the worse for wear. He gave the animal a weak salute as he and the bullfighter headed toward the rails. Jetsam had been good to him, giving him his first decent ride in weeks. His turnaround bull.

At least Emma could now get over the idea that she was jinxing his rides.

The medics quickly checked him over, even though he assured them he hadn't hit his head, and released him, then he headed toward the truck where Emma was pacing. Her chin lifted as she saw him heading toward her, favoring his bruised leg and holding one arm close to his side. Somehow she didn't seem to be as excited as he'd thought she'd be.

"Did LeClair win that one?" he asked in a satisfied voice.

She let out a breath. "He did not. If you hang around tonight, you'll get the check."

"They're mailing it to me." He cocked his head. "Everything okay?"

She gave a slow nod. "It is. Now."

He frowned at her as he realized she was referring to his post-ride dust-up with the bull. "I'm fine. My vest took the brunt of it." He even wore a helmet, which wasn't required of him, because he was born before 1994.

"I know." She spoke matter-of-factly, telling him that

she did indeed know. It wasn't as if she was a rookie to the industry. She was aware of the risks of bull riding.

"What's the deal, Emma?" She gave a small shrug. "You're not back to that jinx thing, are you?" Because he wasn't going to have her taking responsibility for his failures.

She glanced down, keeping her mouth stubbornly shut. He was about to demand that she tell him what was going on, when she brought her gaze back up. "Having a bull randomly kick at you, or throw a hook, is one thing. But seeing a bull roll you on the ground, and then come back for more? Like he was going to take you out? That's...unsettling."

Her voice broke ever so slightly on the last word, making him want to wrap his arms around her, hold her close, show her that he was fine. But that was breaching the rules of the pact, so instead he worked up a smile and said, "You should have seen it from my angle."

Em made a face at him, but her heart wasn't in it, and he once again felt the urge to pull her against him. Hold her. Break their stupid rules.

Instead he said, "Look, Em. I like traveling with you, but if I have to worry about you worrying about me... *that's* a distraction."

She considered his words, then cocked her chin at an angle. "I'm all right."

He didn't think so.

She glanced toward the highway, visible on the opposite side of the rodeo grounds. "We should hit the road if we're going to get any miles behind us tonight."

"I think we should stay here until morning. We can still make the rodeo." It might be close, but they'd get there before his event.

"Why?"

"I'm sore and you're rattled."

Her mouth opened, as if she was going to deny being rattled. He cocked an eyebrow and she closed her mouth.

"Give us both a break, Em."

"All right," she said flatly. The parking lot was clearing of spectators and many of the competitors had already packed up and pulled out. Soon they'd have the place to themselves. "I guess I wouldn't mind an early night."

"And let me buy you dinner instead of raiding your junk food stash."

"My stash is almost empty." She rolled a rock under her boot. "All that's left is the semi-healthy stuff."

"We'll hit a store, replenish your stash, then grab a burger at the café on the edge of town. Get up early and drive."

She frowned at him, her mouth twisting sideways. "Anything else on the agenda?"

"No. That's pretty much it."

The wind gusted as he spoke, knocking his hat sideways and lifting Emma's hair, blowing it around her face. She pushed it back with an impatient hand as Jess righted his hat.

"Storm coming."

"Another reason not to drive tonight." Jess reached out without thinking and tucked a few stray strands of silky red hair behind her ear. He'd just broken the pact, but Emma didn't seem to notice.

"Good point," she said. "I wouldn't mind a burger. And a beer…as long as you're buying."

He smiled. "Just give me a couple minutes to change and I'll see that you have both."

BY THE TIME they returned to the truck and Emma had rolled out her sleeping bag on the rear seat and propped her pillow up against the door, she was mentally exhausted. Jess knew her too well, and even though they'd kept conversation light during dinner, as per the rules of their pact, he'd watched her closely. Read her.

She did not want him to know how deeply affected she'd been by the terrifying conclusion to his ride, but since she'd already given herself away, she'd worked hard for damage control. Jess had laughed at the stories she told about Selma and her brothers, and shared a few Tyler stories, but she felt as if his reactions were merely a cover for what he was really doing, as in, figuring out what was going on with her. Why she'd been close to breaking down when she'd met him at the truck.

She'd like to know that herself.

Emma rolled over and pulled the sleeping bag closer, clutching the soft nylon under her chin. Her heart had stopped when Jess had been tossed through the air after his attempted dismount. And then when the bull went after him…

She squeezed her eyes shut, trying to lose the image. It didn't fade.

Emma rolled over on her back and stared at the ceiling, blinking hard. What the heck? She'd seen Jess have close calls before, and while she'd been heart-in-throat at the time, she recovered as soon as he got to his feet, waved his hand as he always did after a ride.

I don't want to lose him.

Emma pressed her lips together.

That was the truth she'd been sidestepping. She was afraid of losing him. And it wasn't because she loved him as a friend.

Hadn't she learned her lesson with Darion? Get involved with a friend, lose a friend.

She couldn't afford to lose someone else close to her. She shouldn't have continued traveling with Jess. Should have left when she had the chance. Then maybe she wouldn't have crossed this line, allowed herself to start feeling…too much.

Yes. She felt too much. And now she had to do something about it.

Emma dragged in a shuddering breath.

So much for getting her head together while away from home.

Chapter Thirteen

Emma was quiet on the drive to the Big Sky Rodeo. Whatever was going on in her head, she had to deal with on her own, so Jess watched the scenery, told himself to think about his ride.

Instead he thought about Emma. She'd been part of his life forever, but he had a bad feeling that she was slipping away from him. That soon she wouldn't be part of his life.

And there wasn't much he could do about it.

When they reached the rodeo grounds, the grand entry had just started. Jess got out of the truck and headed back to the camper to grab his gear.

"Jess." He looked up to see Em standing near the door. "I'm heading for the stands." She pushed the wind-blown hair back from her face. "Good luck."

He smiled at her. "Thanks, kid."

He stepped into the camper and when he came out again, she was gone. He headed to the rodeo office, opening the door to go in just as Wes reached for the handle to go out. Wes stepped aside to let Jess come into the room, gave him a curt nod and then continued out the door. They hadn't spoken since the night at the bar when Wes had opened up his face with the cue ball, and Jess had no intention of making the first move toward reconciliation. He'd be perfectly happy if he and Wes never spoke again.

He'd pulled another tough bull, which meant he had the potential for another winning ride. Only this time he'd win without scaring Emma.

That was the plan anyway. Dandy did not cooperate.

Jess rode him for eight, but the bull slammed him around, attempted to crush him against the gate, then launched into a spin, reversing course during the final seconds, sucking him down into the well, dislodging him a split second before the buzzer.

Jess jumped to his feet as soon as he hit dirt, ready to run and, sure enough, Dandy made a pass at him with his wicked-looking horns. The bullfighter intervened as Jess made a dash for the fence, clinging to the rails as the bull snorted and raced by. Job done, Dandy headed to the gate and Jess jumped off the fence, so irritated by missing a ride by a fraction of a second that he barely noticed his throbbing shoulder—not until he stooped to pick up his bull rope and it caught fire. He stopped by the medic's trailer briefly, then headed back to the truck where Emma was waiting for him.

She wasn't pale this time. Didn't seem upset. But her shields were up for whatever reason.

"I thought I had this one." He took care not to look as if he was watching her reactions.

"Me, too," Em said, falling in step with him. "You want to drive on tonight?" The question was asked in a polite, distant tone.

Slipping away.

Frustration knotted inside of him. "Yeah. Sounds

good." The next day's rodeo started in the late afternoon and he wanted to be as fresh as possible.

She met his gaze as they walked toward the truck, and for a moment he thought she was about to confess something to him. Then her expression blanked out, which tightened the knot of frustration. *Talk to me, Em.*

He could push things, but he wasn't going to do that.

"I have to take care of a few things, then we can hit the road."

"All right." Em glanced in the direction of the food stands, which were still open for post-rodeo business. "I'll get us something to eat, and meet you back here."

"Sounds good."

Hearing what was on her mind would sound even better, but Em was already gone. In more ways than one.

IT'D BEEN MONTHS since Emma had felt so adrift and unsettled. So alone. Ironically, the guy who understood her best, the guy who could talk her down, was the cause of her unrest.

Jess had insisted on driving that morning, since Emma had driven for several hours the previous evening, getting them halfway to their destination. She didn't feel like knitting as she rode, so instead she focused on the rolling, golden grass-covered hills.

When she returned home, would Darion still be hiding out in Kalispell? And if he'd moved back to Gavin during her absence, would he still avoid her? She'd sent him two texts after their breakup and both had gone unanswered. Either he was truly out of her life, or he wasn't getting her messages. In her heart, she knew the messages had gone through just fine, and that he needed to focus on rebuilding.

She could accept that, but it still stung a little.

Things don't always turn out the way you want them to.

No kidding. If they did, she'd be living a very different life right now. Len would be alive and Selma would be managing Wylie instead of her.

"Hey, Em?"

"I'm okay." She spoke automatically, knowing from his tone that he was going to ask what was up.

"Yeah. Me, too. Now, what's eating you?"

She gave him what she thought was a hard-eyed glare. His gaze didn't waver, so she finally gave up and shifted her gaze to the front again. "I was just going over our situation in my head."

"Meaning the don't-touch-even-if-we-want-to situation?"

"And the wanting-to-stay-friends situation."

"I'm your friend, Em." He spoke with quiet adamancy. "I always will be."

If they left things as they were now, yes, he probably would be. But would she be able to spend any time with him?

It was hard being a friend to a guy who made her ache inside. It was equally hard not to be able to act on that ache. Being distant with Jess didn't feel right…but it felt safe. She needed time and knew instinctively that if she gave in to impulse, things would not end well.

Not only was she not ready, she would not risk her relationship with him. He might get irritated with her standoffishness, but that was a small wound that would heal.

Jess's phone rang and he dug it out of his shirt pocket,

glanced at the screen, then put it to his ear and asked, "What hospital?"

Emma's gaze jerked his way at the mention of a hospital, only to see his lips curve in a fascinating way.

"Hey, it was a legitimate question…yeah. Same to you."

Emma rolled her eyes and settled back in her seat, grateful for the interruption, now that she knew Jess's twin was calling for nonemergency reasons.

She heard the smile in Jess's voice as he said, "Congratulations! That'll help put a roof on your barn," and wondered if Skye, Tyler's wife and her boss, had a hard time dealing with her husband's occupation. She'd never said anything, but maybe Em would ask her sometime.

Or not.

Jess chatted for a few more minutes, then as the town came into sight he said that he had to go and pocketed the phone again.

"Tyler."

"So I gathered."

"Had a huge win."

"Kind of got a hint of that, too."

"That'll be me next year," he said with a cocky smile that looked more Tyler-like than Jess-like.

"I hope it is. I hope you win big."

"So that I'm out of your hair?"

Emma's cheeks started to feel warm. "So that you realize your dream," she said primly.

"I will." He gave her a look she couldn't read. "Trust me on this."

JESS DISAPPEARED SHORTLY after finding a parking spot on the edge of the crowded rodeo grounds. The rodeo had already started, so Emma headed toward the packed stands while he gathered his gear. She shielded her eyes against the sun as she climbed the bleachers, turning her head at the sound of a sharp whistle. Mallory waved at her and Emma started working her way along the row toward where her friend sat.

"Hey, stranger. I didn't know if you were going to be here." Mallory shifted to her left, making room for Emma.

"I didn't see *you* at the last rodeos," Emma said as she sat down.

"Kait picks and chooses. She doesn't have the funds to do every rodeo and sometimes she can't get the time off work."

"Ah." Emma shrugged out of her denim jacket and set it next to her.

"Still traveling with Jess?"

Emma managed a casual smile. "I am. That's why I'm here."

"So, what happened at the Road House? You went to the restroom and never came back."

"I texted you," Emma said with a frown.

"Yes." Mallory leaned closer. "But what happened? We saw the ruckus in the back room, but there were so many people in the hallway that we couldn't tell what was happening."

Emma gave her friend a sideways look. "Long story short? Wes was a jerk, Jess took exception. Wes hit him. Jess hit him back and then someone called the cops so we went out the back door."

"Wow. You escaped. Like Bonnie and Clyde."

"Only without robbing the place."

Mallory shook her head. "I have no idea how you

can travel with that guy and not jump him." Emma frowned at her, hoping she looked perplexed instead of guilty, and Mallory laughed. "I'm sorry. I just know what *I* would do."

Just as Emma knew what she was tempted to do.

What she would not do because she wasn't going to mess up her life again—at least not until she was strong enough to face the consequences.

She and Mallory chatted through the rodeo. Kait clocked the second-fastest time in the barrels and Mallory leaped to her feet, punching the air. "Yes. Gas money!"

Emma laughed—or tried to. The bull-riding event was coming up and her nerves were starting to strum. Mallory continued talking and Emma did her best to follow the conversation while telling herself that she had no reason to be this nervous…except for the fact that Jess hadn't had a truly good ride since they first kissed. Oh, he'd won a couple rodeos, but at what price?

She was not good for him and being on the road was no longer good for her.

When the bull riding started, Mallory stopped talking. The first three rides went well, then Wes got bucked off almost as soon as his bull left the chute. Another good ride followed, then Jess was up, just before LeClair, who would close out the event.

Emma watched him straddle the fence, ease down onto his bull, then realized that her fists were clenched so tightly that her fingers ached. She made a conscious effort to relax her taut muscles only to have them go tight again as the gate opened and Jess's bull burst out into the arena.

Jess was back in form, anticipating the bull's every

twist and turn, sticking to the beast as if he were part of him. It was a beautiful thing to watch, even as her heart hammered.

The whistle blew and Jess tumbled off sideways, with no attempt at finesse, and that was when Emma realized she was standing. She slowly sat down as Jess walked to the gate after giving his customary wave to the crowd.

"Great ride," Mallory said.

Emma waited for her heart to stop trying to pound its way out of her chest before saying, "Yes. He did well."

LeClair was next and by the time he'd finished a ride that rivaled Jess's her heart rate had slowed.

How many times had she watched Jess ride? Dozens if she counted all the rodeos she'd gone to when Len was alive. She'd always felt a touch of anxiety, but nothing like she felt the past two times she'd watched him ride.

And that told her it was more than the ride. More than the fear of losing him. It was…complicated. As if multiple threads had woven together, creating a situation that she didn't understand and didn't know how to address.

"Are you all right?"

Emma turned to Mallory, who had stopped gathering her purse and jacket and was staring at her, an expression of concern creasing her forehead.

"Actually," Emma said slowly, "I don't know."

"What's wrong?"

"It's a very long story."

"I have a very long evening ahead of me. Kait has a boyfriend and I probably won't see her until the wee hours."

People around them were getting to their feet, gathering belongings. Emma and Mallory stood to make it easier for people to get by. Emma met Mallory's gaze as the last guy eased by, but couldn't bring herself to say yes. Did she really want to share? If she talked about it, then the situation would become more...real.

As if it wasn't real now.

"It had to do with your bull rider, right?"

Her bull rider. Emma moistened her lips. "Yeah." She sat back down as the announcer started naming the winners. "My bull rider, whom I want to keep as a friend."

Mallory jerked her head toward the stairs. "Come with me. We'll get a drink somewhere and you can tell me as much or as little as you want."

Emma got to her feet. A drink sounded good. A sounding board even better. Maybe she did need to get some of this out in the open. Get a second opinion. Stop pretending that staring out the window would give her an answer, when experience told her it wouldn't.

JESS WAS LOADING his gear into the truck when the text from Emma came in.

Out with Mallory. Back in an hour or two.

Jess tapped out a quick reply and then opened the tiny fridge to pull out a beer before pulling his notebook off the shelf above the bunk and settling at the table. He wasn't going to make the mistake of going after her again. If she got into trouble, she had friends.

He flipped open the cover and scanned the calendar he'd taped just inside. Five more rodeos. He noted the name of the bull he rode and his score and was about to close the book when he instead opened to the pages where he'd outlined his plan. He read through it, then closed the book, took another pull from the bottle.

Funny how the bad rides had made him more determined to bring his plan to fruition. He'd get through this season and then attempt to go pro regardless of how he finished. If he failed, he failed, and at least he'd know.

In for a dime, in for a dollar, as Ty always said. Ty had done well following that advice, and there was no reason Jess couldn't be just as successful. He was committed now. More so than when he started.

He leaned his head back and closed his eyes. When he jerked awake again, the camper was dark and his neck was stiff. And his first thought was to wonder whether Emma had made it back yet.

Scooting out from behind the table, he made his way out of the camper, rubbing his stiff neck as he walked around the truck. He glanced in the window as he walked by on the way to the facilities, saw Emma's boots sitting on the front seat where she always left them, along with her clothing, while she slept, and instantly felt better. She was back.

Back, but still shut off from him.

He missed her. Missed her smart mouth and sassy comebacks. Missed having her drive him crazy by doing things like telling the biggest gossip on the circuit that they were on their honeymoon.

Good times.

When he got back to the camper, Jess stripped down to his boxer briefs and climbed into the bunk, where he lay staring at the dark ceiling. Sure, he could have fallen asleep sitting up a couple hours ago, but now...

A light tap on the door brought him onto one elbow. Before he could push the covers back, Emma opened the door and stepped inside. Jess went still, half afraid that if he moved or spoke, she would head back out, and he didn't want that. Not until he knew why she was there. Why she was in essence breaking the pact.

If that jerk, Wes, had done anything to her…

The thought evaporated as Em started toward him. When she reached the bunk, she eased herself onto it. Almost but not quite touching him.

"Em?"

She touched him then. Brushed his face with her fingers before lowering herself down beside him, her knees making contact with his.

Jess almost forgot to breathe. Still propped on his elbow, he gently touched her face with his free hand, smoothing her hair away from her cheek, wondering what was going on. She skimmed her fingers along his jawline, sending a primal need surging through him before she settled her head to his pillow and nestled up against him. Jess studied her profile against his pillow, grateful that she was there, confused as to the reason.

Finally, he dropped a protective hand over her, gathered her closer and settled in.

"What's going on, Em?"

"I'm leaving."

He pulled back so that he could see her face in the dim light. "When?"

"Tomorrow. I can't do this anymore."

He gently caressed her face. "Do what?"

"My being here isn't doing either of us any good. It's distracting you from your rides."

"I won tonight."

"You could have done better."

He was ready to take offense when it struck him that

she was clinging to the bad rides as a reason to leave, rather than deal with the real issue. Which put him in the position of having to make a choice.

"Would it be so horrible to hook up with me?" Because she was there. In his arms. In his bed. Which told him that she didn't find him repulsive.

"I'm not ready for a committed relationship." She whispered the words against his bare chest and he felt her squeeze her eyes shut, as if the admission hurt.

"What would make you ready?"

He hoped that she would say, "Time." Didn't happen. She drew in a breath and said, "I don't know if I'll ever be ready." He felt her hand, which was trapped between them, close into a fist. "I'm afraid of wanting…and I'm afraid of losing."

"Losing what?" He threaded his fingers through her hair, letting the silky strands slide over his palm.

"You. Me."

His fingers stilled for a moment. "That doesn't make a lot of sense."

"I'll screw it up if I dive in now. Just as I screwed up pretty much everything since Len died." She pulled away again, looking him in the eye as she said, "Trust me… it's best for both of us. You'll get your mojo back—"

"It's already back."

"And I'll take my life back."

Jess let out a sigh of his own. "Yet you're here in my bed." Right where he'd wanted her to be for the past weeks.

"Only to say goodbye."

He pulled her closer, settling his cheek against the top of her head, and wished that she wasn't in a position to be so utterly aware of her effect on him.

She released a shaky breath, her body going stiff as she said, "I was thinking of goodbye in a nonverbal sense."

Her meaning crashed into him. She wanted to sleep with him. Wanted to make love before leaving, thus stretching his resolve close to the breaking point. He dug deep for the strength he needed. "You'll regret it, Em."

Her eyes were wide and earnest as she said, "I won't. I want…something."

"But not everything."

"I can't risk losing you, Jess, and I'm afraid that'll happen if I commit before I'm ready."

Because that was what had happened with Darion. Jess closed his eyes, willed himself to stay strong. Em had issues to work out. And the only way he could help was to be there for her…but not in the way she was asking for tonight. He couldn't handle making love to her and then having her leave.

"You can stay with me tonight, but I'm not making love to you. Not the way things are right now."

She let out a soft breath against his chest. "You're sure."

No, he wasn't. But this was Em. He smoothed his hand over her back, glad that she was wearing her T-shirt and sweatpants, because if they were skin to skin, he may not have had the willpower to say, "Yes, Emma. I'm sure. Do you still want to stay?"

She nodded against his chest. "Just for a bit. Then I'll go."

Jess eventually dozed off and when he woke, his bunk was empty. Emma had slipped away. He lay wide-awake until the sky lightened and then he got up, dressed and went to find Em.

She was sitting in the front seat of the truck, staring straight ahead. He opened the door and for a silent moment they faced off. When she turned to face him, her face was pale and there were shadows under her beautiful eyes. Why had it taken him so damned long to see just how beautiful she was? Inside. Outside. Why hadn't he come to her after Len passed? Then he could have helped her through the rough times.

"Wylie will be here soon."

"He must have gotten an early start."

"He was in Livingston already."

"Handy."

She shrugged. "Jess…"

"We'll talk later." He wasn't going to let her slip completely out of his life without a word or two being exchanged, but this wasn't the time. Her head came up and he followed her gaze, spotting a familiar Dodge Power Wagon pulling off the highway.

He turned back to Emma, who was now looking at him instead of her brother's truck. She pressed her lips together, doing her best to mask the emotions he could read so easily. She was protecting herself, and until she no longer felt the need to do that, there wasn't much he could do. So he'd say goodbye, finish his season.

But he wouldn't stop thinking about her.

Wylie pulled into the lot too fast and roared up close to them. Jess reached out to slide his hand behind Emma's neck, cupping the back of her head as he lowered his head to give her a last kiss goodbye.

"I didn't mean to fall in love with you."

Her eyes went wide and her lips parted just as Wylie

leaped out of the truck, slamming the door behind him. He gave her another quick kiss, noted that her lips clung to his just a little too long, then stepped back.

"Hey, Wylie." He lifted his hand to Emma's brother, then, because he really didn't feel like shooting the breeze, turned and headed off toward the tiny café across the street from the rodeo grounds.

He wasn't hungry in the least, but he was not going to watch her drive away.

Chapter Fourteen

Wylie kept giving Emma strange sideways looks as they headed back home. At first Emma ignored them, but then, because he showed no signs of relenting, she said, "We're not involved."

"Yeah. It sure came off that way." He gave her another look, which came off as both accusatory and protective. That was all she needed—Wylie in protect-o mode.

Emma tightened her jaw. "All right. We're totally involved. That's why I called you in the middle of the night and asked for a ride home. Because I want to escape the guy I'm involved with."

"Mom thinks you're going off the deep end."

"No doubt. So maybe you could do me a favor and not give her any more ammunition."

"Like I would."

Emma rolled her eyes. He wouldn't—until Selma sat him down for a good grilling. Then he'd spill in order to escape. Wylie was the baby of the family. Eighteen and the only one still living at home, meaning the only kid that Selma got to manage full-time.

They fell into silence and Emma stared out at the passing scenery, feeling strangely empty. Numb. Which was crazy because she and Jess hadn't even done anything. She'd offered herself up and Jess had refused.

How was she supposed to take that?

Maybe he wasn't a one-night-stand kind of guy… Although she knew better because she'd heard girls talking about the Hayward twins. Mostly Ty, but Jess's name had come up.

What would it have been like sleeping with him? Probably better than anything she'd ever experienced before in that realm.

And she'd walked away from the guy.

What choice had she had? She wasn't ready for a relationship. Wasn't ready to feel pinned down. She was too young to be pinned down. Wasn't that why she'd broken up with Darion? Because she'd wanted excitement in her life.

Emma pressed her forehead to the window. None of her justifications were ringing true, except for not being ready for a relationship. She wasn't ready to take the risk, face the consequences of things going wrong.

"Some stuff happened while you were gone."

"Yeah?"

"Archer started dating Wendy Tarrington."

"Oooh." Emma grimaced. "How did Selma take that?"

"About the way you'd expect. Dad tried to tell her that Archer wasn't that serious. And he wasn't. I don't think…"

That was something, for her dad to take a stand of sorts. She imagined that he got about halfway through his sentence before Selma took over. But in this case, Selma was right. Wendy had a scorched earth policy with men. She got everything she could out of them and then moved on. Knowing Archer, he probably thought he was in control of the relationship.

"What happened?"

"Exactly what Selma told Arch would happen. Wendy drained his bank account and moved on."

"How's Arch?"

Wylie smiled with grim humor. "Older. Wiser. Broke."

"Good lesson to learn young."

"Yeah. If I date anyone Mom doesn't like, I'm going to keep it a secret."

A sputtering laugh burst from Emma's lips and Wylie smiled back. It was silly to think that any kind of a secret could be kept from their mom.

"She means well," Wylie said.

She did. But meaning well didn't mean she was right about everything.

"Her protective gene is strong," Emma said tactfully. And had gotten worse since Len had died.

"How about DJ? Still hitting the books?"

Her middle brother had tried to drop out of college after his first year, only to run into a roadblock named Selma.

"Finished his summer courses last week."

"Imagine that." Emma smiled. It was kind of fun watching her brothers fight for autonomy. It made her feel less alone against Selma.

As they approached Gavin, Wylie shot her yet another look, only this one was edged with concern and something that looked strikingly like empathy. "Do you want me to drop you off at Howard's motel?"

Emma shook her head. "I'm done hiding."

"Are you going to the ranch?"

"I didn't say I was walking into the lion's den. I'm just not going to run." She lifted her chin. "Skye is letting me live in the trailer on her place until I get another apartment." Which hopefully wouldn't take long, because Skye was married to Jess's twin. The only reason she'd agreed to the arrangement, which her boss had put forth when Em had called to see about being put back onto the work schedule at the café the previous evening, was because Ty was on the road and Skye hoped to join him. She could watch the place for a week or two while she found somewhere to live.

"Okay. The Larkin Ranch. If Mom asks—"

"*When* she asks, tell her where I'm living and tell her that I'll call and set up a time when we can talk. And tell her that she's not to contact me before I contact her."

Wylie frowned at her. "You're sure about that?" he asked dubiously.

"Very." Until she got a grip on all the stuff in her life that was driving her crazy, she'd never truly have control of anything.

"What about Dad?"

"I'll call his cell. Let him know I got back in one piece." Even though she really hadn't.

AFTER EM LEFT with her brother, Jess had driven to his next rodeo on autopilot, barely aware of the passing miles as he debated about how to deal with a situation he didn't know how to fix.

One that he suspected couldn't be fixed.

Not now anyway. Emma had faced too much loss in too short of a time and wasn't going to risk more. She'd been willing to sleep with him to say goodbye, but Jess wasn't going to do that to himself. He needed more than a goodbye romp and Emma couldn't handle more. Which left them at an impasse. Emma afraid to risk losing more than she'd already lost, and Jess wanting more than she could give.

He couldn't do anything right now. He had to wait until she was ready.

And when might that be?

Hell, he didn't know. But it wasn't now. If he pushed, he'd lose her.

You've already lost her.

Jess shifted his weight behind the steering wheel, trying to find a comfortable spot. His knee ached, his shoulder throbbed. He barely noticed as he sorted through the charred remains of his doomed road trip—a trip that was supposed to give Emma breathing room, but had, instead, complicated both of their lives.

He kept replaying their last encounter. Maybe he should have said goodbye in the way she'd wanted. Maybe if he had, things would be different now...

No. They wouldn't.

His gut knotted. How in the world was he supposed to fix this?

By the time he reached the rodeo grounds, he was beyond tense. He checked into his event, prepped his rope, stretched taut muscles. Then he got onto his bull as if riding the beast was a routine chore he needed to complete before closing shop for the day. The bull did his best, but Jess did better, scoring a ninety.

The win felt excellent, but not nearly as good as it would have felt if Em had been there to tell him that LeClair had really won.

TWO DAYS AFTER she returned from her road trip, Emma's father drove his rattletrap old truck into Larkin Ranch and parked it beside the trailer she now called home. Emma dropped the curtain she'd pulled aside when she'd heard the familiar chug of the old diesel engine and hurried to the door. What the heck?

She'd called her dad not long after Wylie had dropped her off, assured him that she was back for good and told him that she'd see him at the ranch in a week or two. Davis Sullivan, being a man of few words, had simply said, "Looking forward to it." He hadn't said anything about meeting up with her and it was so out of character that Emma's heart started beating faster as he got out of the truck. Had something happened at home? Were the boys all right? Selma? She hated to think of how adrift her dad would be without his strong-willed wife.

"Hey," he said simply, an easy smile on his face.

Okay. No emergency. Emma held the door open and smiled back. "Come on in. See my new digs."

He walked past her into the trailer that Jess's brother had once called home. Stopped and looked around. "Not as nice as your bedroom on the ranch, but it'll do."

"Want some coffee?" She waved her dad to the table. He nodded before sitting. Emma found an extra cup and poured, topping off her own cup before sitting on the opposite side of the small table.

"Is everything all right?"

"That's what I came to find out."

Emma gave him a perplexed look. "I'm fine."

"Just wanted to make sure." He lifted his cup and took a drink. "Selma's convinced that you aren't."

"I am. I needed to get away."

"I'd say that's pretty obvious, Em. Everything go all right on the road?"

Emma tipped her chin as she regarded her father. How much did he know? What had Wylie said? The last thing she wanted was for Dad to be worried about her. "Actually…yes. I learned a few things. I'm glad I went."

Sometimes. At other times, she felt positively bruised by the experience. She hadn't lost Jess's friendship, but what good did that do her when she couldn't handle being near him?

"Selma says you sent her a message via Wylie, that you'd set the time and place for the first meeting."

Emma lifted her coffee cup and sipped casually, glad that he'd brushed by the subject of the road trip. "I don't want to rehash old business before I'm ready. I want a week or two to settle in, then I'll come to the ranch."

"That sounds fair."

Emma frowned over her cup. "Do you mean that?"

Davis gave a slow nod. "She's pretty busy trying to iron out Archer's life right now. We wouldn't want to heap too much on an already full plate."

For a moment, Emma stared at her dad, wondering if he had meant to make a joke. The gentle crinkling at the corners of his eyes told her, yes, he had. Wow.

"I know she means well."

"She does."

"Dad…" Emma chose her words carefully. "Do *you* think I'm old enough to live my own life?"

"I don't know that any parent feels good letting go… especially after losing a child."

Emma reached out and took hold of his wrist and squeezed. "I know."

"Selma wants you settled. She wants all of you settled. Then she'll feel like her job is done."

"Really, Dad?"

Again, the corners of his eyes crinkled. "That's what
she thinks. Now."

But they both knew better.

Emma cleared her throat before asking the hard question. "Why didn't you stand up for me when Selma was
harassing me to get back with Darion?" Her dad was a
retiring guy, but still…

Davis glanced down at the table, his mouth flatten-
ing. "I'm embarrassed to say that I didn't realize the full
extent of the situation. I was busy in the fields and…
dealing with…stuff."

His son's death.

Emma was quiet for a moment. "I can understand
that."

He raised his eyes. "I'm feeling…better. Being alone
made it easier to cope."

"Like being with Darion made it easier for me to
cope."

"Which was another reason I think Selma couldn't
accept your breakup."

"She made it sound as if it was all about the dress."

"She's still kind of hot about the dress," he admitted.
"But she'll cool off. Eventually."

"What else has been going on while I was gone?"

"Where to begin?" Her dad continued to drink his
coffee as he filled her in on his new bull purchase and
gave her a rundown of Archer's misadventure with
Wendy Tarrington. After finishing his coffee, he pushed
his chair back.

"I'm on my way to the ranch supply store, so I'd better get going. I just wanted to see you."

"I'm glad you did." Emma walked with her dad to the door. "Does Selma know you were going to stop by?"

"No. But I'll tell her you're looking good."

Emma nodded, running a hand up the edge of the door after she pulled it open. "I'll be out to the ranch in a week or two."

"I'll make sure she doesn't give you an unexpected visit before you're ready."

"You can do that?" The words came out before she considered the implications—she hadn't meant to imply that he didn't have a say in his relationship, even if that was the feeling she had. But her dad didn't seem one bit insulted. Instead he gave her a slow smile.

"Emma…you might be surprised at what I can do."

"I…uh… Right."

Davis winked at her, then headed for his truck, leaving Emma to wonder if she had any idea at all of what the true relationship was between her father and her stepmother.

THE SOUND OF boots on gravel coming up fast behind him made Jess glance over his shoulder.

Tim LeClair. Tim was a decent guy and a gracious competitor. He was also behind Jess in the money. Despite having Emma on the brain and more often than not driving all night to make his next rodeo. Jess was on a winning streak. Emma had been gone for about a week, and he'd crammed in all the rodeos that he could—traveling to Idaho, as well as following the Montana circuit—and winning most of them. He'd decided to continue onto the next leg of the rodeo circuit instead of returning home to Gavin for few days, like he'd originally planned.

"Nice ride."

Jess looked over his shoulder to see Tim LeClair a few yards behind him, chaps in one hand, gear bag in the other.

"Thanks." He waited for Tim to fall into step with him as they headed to the competitors' lot, where they were parked side by side.

Since Jess no longer had a driver to share road duties, he and Tim had tossed around the idea of traveling together, but hadn't set up any kind of official plan. Mainly because Jess wasn't yet certain he wanted to lose the freedom of having his own wheels—just in case he had the sudden urge to head back to Gavin. There was only one reason for him to do that, and that reason had yet to be in contact with him.

Ty had called the previous evening and mentioned that she'd be watching the place while Skye spent her vacation days on tour with him. Ty appeared to assume that ranch-sitting was the reason Emma had returned home, and Jess did nothing to clue his twin in to the truth. Ty did dig a little, asking about how traveling with Em had been, and Jess had given what he hoped was a suitably casual answer. It'd been all right. He hated to lose his driver.

He'd pretty much lied. There was nothing casual about his feelings toward Em.

He and Tim continued to their rigs in silence, Tim limping a little and Jess holding his arm close to his bruised side. But they were both mobile and cognizant of their surroundings, which meant it had been a good day.

They parted ways at the trucks and Jess climbed into his camper to make a quick sandwich before driving on that night. Emma hadn't spent all that much time in the camper, so it shouldn't feel unusually empty every time he went inside, but it did.

There was a knock on the door and Jess called out that it was open. Tim stuck his head in.

"Want to finalize some travel plans?"

It only made sense. They were both heading to a large-purse rodeo in Wyoming to fill an empty niche in the schedule, passing though Gavin on the way.

It was time.

"Yeah, let's do that." The solitary driving was beginning to wear and he was spending too much time alone. In his head. Feeling both protective and helpless where Em was concerned.

"My sister has a place near West Yellowstone," Tim said. "We can stop there before heading into Wyoming, then drive north after the rodeo and pick things back up in Circle. The only question is, do we drop your rig in Gavin, or mine in West Yellowstone?"

"I'll drop mine. Your camper is bigger." And newer. And it didn't remind him of Em.

During the weeks following her return home, Emma established a routine that kept her busy. Instead of driving from rodeo to rodeo, she drove from the Larkin Ranch to the café. She only had a part-time schedule to begin with, but she covered for people who needed extra time off, so she was there almost every day. When she wasn't at the café, she hung out with Skye and learned the ranch routine so that she could care for the place while Skye was on the road. She liked living on the

Larkin Ranch, liked caring for the livestock and helping in Skye's garden. The trailer she rented was roomy enough that she didn't feel cramped, and if she wanted company, Skye was there.

The only sticking point was the fact that Skye's husband was Jess's twin, Tyler.

But Tyler wasn't there and had no plans to arrive anytime soon. Skye was due to fly out the following weekend to meet him in Texas, and Emma wasn't sure about how she felt about having the ranch to herself. Too much alone time meant too much thinking time and at the moment, she was trying very hard not to think about Jess. Or the way she'd left him.

Or him saying that he hadn't intended to fall in love with her.

No. She wasn't going to think about those things. Wasn't going to think about Jess. And for hours at a time she sometimes succeeded in that endeavor.

Okay…more like half hours at a time.

The guy was in her brain and under her skin.

And as Emma left the barn after feeding the goose that lived there, he also appeared to be standing in the driveway next to the house. Emma almost dropped the feed bucket, before she realized she was staring at Tyler, not Jess.

Tyler, who was supposed to be on the other side of the country.

"Sorry about that," he said when she got closer.

Emma felt the color rise in her cheeks, wondering just how transparent her emotions had been. "What?"

"You thought I was Jess."

Very transparent. "What if I did?"

He narrowed his eyes at her. "It appeared to mean something to you…seeing my brother."

She moistened her lips, bought some time, then went with the truth. "He does mean something to me."

"Just not enough?"

"Tyler!"

They turned together to see Skye standing on the porch a few feet away, frowning at her husband. Emma didn't know how much she'd heard, but it seemed as if she'd heard enough to feel as if she needed to rescue Em.

Em turned back to Ty and met his appraising look with one of her own. It was unnerving seeing someone who looked so much like Jess, but wasn't Jess. But if she'd been this close to Jess, her heart would have been beating faster, as it had during that split second she'd thought Ty was his twin.

"Maybe you should mind your business, not your brother's," she finally said. "As tempting as it might be to fly in and protect him, he's doing okay on his own."

A slow smile transformed Ty's face as Skye came to stand beside him, linking her arm through his. He winced as she touched his side. "Easy, babe."

"Oh, yeah. You're going to climb on a bull in a week and I need to be easy with you."

Emma grabbed the distraction Skye had offered with both hands. "Where are you competing?"

Ty cocked an eyebrow at her, indicating that he knew she was sidestepping, before saying, "We're off to Houston for a special Man vs. Bull event."

"However, my husband got himself mashed last night, so decided to fly home for a few days of rest and recuperation." Skye couldn't quite disguise the fact that she totally adored the guy, and Emma felt an odd pang of jealousy.

"Sounds...fun." She lifted the feed bucket. "I should finish the chores."

"You want to have dinner with us? I made a stew. There's plenty."

Emma started shaking her head apologetically before Skye finished talking. She was not going to hang with Jess's brother. It was simply too unsettling. Made her too aware of what felt very much like unfinished business. "I have some stuff I need to work on...and I'm gearing up for my big meeting with Selma tomorrow."

"Ah. The showdown."

Tyler frowned, but Emma didn't feel like explaining. Skye could fill him in. "Tomorrow is the mutually agreed upon day." She'd actually tried to meet a few days earlier, but Selma had been adamant that it had to be on Saturday. So Emma had waited for Saturday. She figured she'd choose her battles and day of the week wasn't one of them.

"If you get hungry, the invitation stands."

Emma took care not to look at Tyler as she said, "Thank you. I'll keep that in mind."

As it turned out, she didn't need to take advantage of her invitation, because Skye knocked on the door to the trailer a little after sundown. When Emma opened it, Skye held out a covered dish.

"I brought you stew. I thought you might need some hearty food as you prepare for battle."

Emma laughed and reached for the dish. Skye gave it to her, but she didn't move. Something was up.

"What?" Emma asked simply, holding the warm bowl with both hands.

"Since you're going to your ranch, and I'm pretty sure you're going to notice when you drive by Jess's trailer… He came back to drop his truck off at his place about a week ago."

"Oh." The word came out sounding normal, but Emma was glad that she didn't have to say much more. Jess had been back. Without so much as a call or a text.

Of course, he was under no obligation to contact her. If he'd asked to see her, she would have said no. So what the heck? Why did it feel like a knife had just twisted inside of her?

"He's sharing a ride with another bull rider," Skye said.

Emma moistened her lips. "That makes sense. I'm glad to hear he's sharing. I kind of left him hanging."

"Why did you do that?"

The unasked question that had been hanging between them had suddenly been asked—in a gentle way, but asked all the same.

"I…didn't know what else to do."

Skye nodded. "I wish I had some amazing words of wisdom."

Emma smiled a little. "Me, too. But I don't think there are any words. And, right now, I have to focus on establishing my independence where my stepmom is involved."

"One battle at a time."

"Exactly." She sounded strong. In control. The opposite of what she felt.

"I have to go in early tomorrow, so I'll wish you luck now," Skye said.

"Thank you." Emma held up the bowl of stew. "And thank you for dinner."

"The least I could do."

A few seconds later, Skye was gone, the door was closed and Emma was alone in her trailer. She placed the stew on the table and then hugged her arms around her as she dropped her head back to stare up at the ceiling.

Jess had come back to Gavin. And he hadn't told her.

That spoke volumes. In her quest not to ruin a friendship, she'd done exactly that. Even if she hadn't killed it outright, she'd dealt it a mortal blow.

And it was killing her.

Chapter Fifteen

As Emma drove into the family ranch, she wondered yet again why Selma had been so accommodating about her request for some time before they met. Because that wasn't the way Selma rolled, Emma had spent the last fourteen days ping-ponging back and forth between theories. She figured that maybe going on the road with Jess had finally convinced her stepmom that Emma was old enough to go her own way…or she was merely playing nice to lull her into a sense of false security before trying to take over again.

When Emma pulled around the barn and headed for her usual parking spot, only to find it filled with a very familiar vehicle, she instantly realized why her stepmother had been so reasonable about setting up a meeting on a specific date.

It had given her time to set up an ambush.

Emma's breath quickened as she parked next to Darion's truck and turned off the engine, then she slammed the door a little too hard as she got out of her car.

Really? He'd totally sidestepped any contact with her and now he was here, doing Selma's bidding?

Emma walked in through the back door, because Selma would have expected her to enter by the front.

The back door was used only for coming and going during chores. She crossed the neat kitchen with its black-and-white tile floor, old, yet shiny appliances and large scarred-up family dining table. How many family fights had broken out at the table? And how many family celebrations and gatherings held there? Len's wake popped into her head, but she pushed the thought aside. Families were complicated, and she was about to simplify her life.

When she walked into the living room the first thing she saw was Darion sitting on the leather sofa, looking very much as if he wanted to be anywhere except for on the Sullivan family ranch. That worked because Emma was about to send him on his way before she and her stepmom got into things.

Selma jumped to her feet as soon as Emma entered the room, her welcoming smile fading when she saw the fiery look on her stepdaughter's face.

Emma stopped dead center in the room, looking at first Selma and then Darion. "I don't know what's going on, but I'm not in the mood for a surprise attack."

Darion had the grace to go red, as did Selma, but not for the same reasons. Emma walked past her stepmother and stopped in front of Darion, who got to his feet.

"Em—"

She raised her hands in a warning gesture and he closed his mouth again. "I think you should go."

"But—" Selma started to speak, then stopped abruptly when Emma whirled on her.

"No buts," Emma said through clenched teeth. She turned back to Darion. "I'm sorry if you traveled far, but this is not the place where we are going to have our first post-breakup discussion."

"Yeah," he said with a quick nod before shooting a dark look at Selma. "I agree."

Without another word, he headed for the front door, leaving Selma and Emma facing off. Neither said a word until they heard the truck door open and close and the engine start.

"Well, now you've done it," Selma muttered.

Emma gaped at her. Gaped and grasped for the logic…and then she laughed. It was all so ridiculous.

"It's not funny," Selma snapped. "He's a good man."

"I know he is," Emma said as she sank down in a floral upholstered chair. One thing Selma was good at was making a house seem like a home—and it was a *good* home, as long as a person was willing to play things her way. Or had the backbone to stand up to her. "But he's not the man for me."

Selma took a few paces, then turned, her arms folded over her middle. "Why not?"

They'd taken a few stabs at this conversation before, but matters had quickly degenerated into anger and defensiveness. The dress. The deposits. The fact that Emma was making poor choices for her future.

Emma pulled in a long breath and took a moment to study the woman who had raised her. "Selma. Mom. The thing is…marrying me off doesn't mean that you've successfully completed your task."

"What does that mean?"

Emma gripped the arms of her chair. Even though Selma had the height advantage, she remained seated. "It means that's what this whole thing has felt like." And her conversation with her dad had verified her theory. "You aren't paying attention to the fact that, good man or not, I don't want to marry Darion. And he doesn't want to marry me. Why would you persist in hounding us if it wasn't for your own peace of mind."

Selma let out a tiny huff and threw up her hands. "Well, my peace of mind does play into it. Make no mistake there."

Emma frowned at her.

Selma took a couple of paces then turned back. "I almost didn't marry your father, you know."

Emma blinked at her. "No. I didn't."

"Well, I came that close—" she held up her thumb and forefinger "—from making the biggest mistake of my life. Because I thought that maybe I wanted more than he could offer. I had nerves. Plain and simple. And so did you."

Emma rolled her eyes. "I did not have an attack of nerves. I had an attack of reality. I'm glad you married Dad. But it's not the same thing."

"How is it different?" Selma challenged.

"Darion and I are friends. Were friends." She didn't know what they were now. "How did you get him here?"

"It wasn't easy," Selma sniffed. "But I thought if the two of you were brought together. Had a chance to talk…"

"I don't want Darion." She didn't. She wasn't even sure if she wanted him as a friend after this ambush… although, in his defense, Selma was hard to say no to.

Selma turned on her. "Then what do you want?"

Emma didn't see where what she wanted was any of Selma's business, but, in the name of ending her step-mom's meddling, she said, "I want to be in control of my life. I want to answer to myself and only myself. I want to make choices for my life that only involve me."

A brittle silence followed her words and then Selma gave a snort. "Sounds pretty selfish to me."

It sounded selfish to Emma, too. And not even remotely true.

She didn't want to live her life alone. She'd spent so much time dodging Selma that it seemed as if that was what she wanted, but…was it really?

She raised her eyes to her stepmom and said the words in her heart. "I don't want to live under a microscope. I don't want to be micromanaged. I don't want to marry to escape grief or feel safe or to have an ally against you…sorry." She pressed her lips together, but Selma only rolled her eyes. Okay. She hadn't mortally wounded her stepmom.

"I know I'm tough—"

"And intrusive. I love you, but, Mom…give me some room to breathe."

Selma regarded the family photo on the wall above Emma's head. "Room to breathe."

"Yes."

Selma gave her an appraising sidelong look. "Kind of dramatic, don't you think?"

"No. I don't want my choices made for me." Emma closed her eyes, tightened her lips. When her eyes came open again, she said, "If I'm about to step off a cliff, stop me, but otherwise, let me make my own mistakes."

"I'm trying to help," Selma muttered. She gave a sniff and sat on the edge of the sofa. "Life isn't easy."

Emma sat on the other end of the sofa, half turning to face her stepmom. "Losing Len taught me that."

"I don't want you kids to hurt."

Emma reached out and touched her stepmother's hand. "You can't control those kinds of things. You'll get an ulcer if you try."

"Already have one." Selma's mouth instantly tight

ened and she gave Emma a fierce look as if daring her to comment.

Emma scowled back. "For how long?"

Selma waved a hand. "Davis made me go to the doctor a couple of months ago."

"He made you?" There was definitely more to the dynamic of her father and stepmother's relationship than she'd been aware of. And this was probably what Wylie had been referring to when he'd told her early in the road trip that Selma wasn't acting like herself.

"I wouldn't have gone otherwise." Selma's hand clenched into a fist.

"Do the boys know about this?"

Selma frowned at her. "Of course not."

"That's it. You need to focus on something other than us."

Selma raised a startled gaze. "But—"

Emma held up a hand, cutting her stepmom off. "No more ex-fiancé attacks." Selma opened her mouth and Em waved her finger. "Let Archer learn his women lessons the hard way. Make Wylie do his own laundry."

"He doesn't understand stain removal."

"Then he'll wear dirty jeans. Consequences, Selma. Let them happen. Don't try to fix everything. Run everything." She drew in a breath that made her shoulders rise. "Let Dad carry some of the burden."

"I've never…"

Emma stuck her chin out. "*Do* it. When your ulcer is better, we'll revisit. And I want a doctor's note giving you the all clear." Emma got to her feet. "I'll talk to Wylie and Archer and DJ. You might be able to take us one at a time, but I don't think you can fight a united front."

"For heaven's sake, Em. I'm not an invalid."

"And it kind of sucks losing control of one's life, right?"

Selma blinked at Emma as the meaning of her words sank in. "This isn't the same."

"It is." She pulled out her phone. "I'll just call the boys in from the fields and we're going to have a family meeting."

EMMA DROVE BACK to town almost two hours after she'd arrived at the ranch thinking that the world was a strange place. She'd gone home hell-bent on establishing autonomy and ended up in a family meeting about her stepmom's health.

There was no way Selma was going to let her family call all the shots, but once Archer, DJ and Wylie were apprised of the situation, they let it be known that, yes, they thought their mother worried about them too much—*worry* being code for *control*, of course—and they wanted her to focus on getting well.

Several times during the discussion, Selma had raised her gaze to meet that of her husband, who'd stood behind the kitchen table where his sons and wife sat, his arms folded over his chest. Every single time Davis had nodded his agreement with what Emma or her brothers had said, Selma bit her lip as if making a conscious effort to listen to her family instead of fighting back. Or maybe she was plotting strategy. Whatever the reason, there were five of them and one of her and it was the first time that her family had ever presented a united front against her...for her own good.

Emma didn't believe for one minute that Selma would instantly reform, but she thought that perhaps

she and her brothers might be able to handle her inter-
ference in a different way than before. And that maybe
they understood things a little better. When she'd left,
her dad had sat down next to Selma and put a hand on
her shoulder as he leaned close to hear what she had to
say. Emma had seen them do that before, but had always assumed that Selma was giving orders.

Maybe not.

Maybe things were not always as they appeared—or
as she'd decided they were.

DARION'S TRUCK WAS parked near the diner when Emma
drove back through town on her way to the Larkin
Ranch. She pulled her truck into a space on the next
block. Now she wasn't going to have to hunt him down.
She and Darion had a few issues to iron out.

His head came up as she walked through the diner
door, almost as if he'd been expecting her, and when
she stopped next to his table he waved her into the other
side of the booth. Emma slid across the vinyl seat and
he motioned for her friend Chloe to bring coffee—just
like old times. Except that this wasn't old times.

"I'm sorry." His mouth tightened ruefully as he
cupped the heavy ceramic coffee mug in front of him
with both hands. Strong hands, like Jess's, but she'd
never found them as fascinating.

"What happened?"

He shrugged self-consciously. "Selma. She told me
that you needed me."

Emma leaned back as Chloe put a cup in front of her,
filled it and then topped off Darion's coffee. Emma sent
her a quick smile, then settled back to business. "Did
she elaborate?"

"She was just mysterious enough that I felt as if I had to come. As if you really did need me."

There was something in his tone that made her cock her head ever so slightly. "Do you need me to need you?"

He shrugged before candidly meeting her gaze. "It's what brought us together, held us together."

"Until we came to our senses."

He nodded. "When Selma called, the old protective instinct kicked in."

"You've been avoiding me."

"Yeah." His cheeks colored as he dropped his gaze to his cup. He was a great-looking guy with warm hazel eyes and sun-streaked brown hair, and his tendency toward shyness made him all the more endearing. But she'd never longed for him, never felt the ache for him. She'd needed him after the accident that killed Len, had trusted him, loved him, but she hadn't *wanted* him in the way a wife should want her husband.

He lifted his chin. "I thought it was best for both of us. And the texts you sent...they seemed like duty texts."

Now Emma's cheeks warmed. "They were, in a way."

"I was afraid that if we got back together, we might fall back into old habits." He leaned back, still cupping the mug on the table. "But it appears that you're back in fighting form."

"I wouldn't say that. But I've grown. Figured a few things out." Unfortunately, she still had a few issues to sort through. And they were the big ones.

"I met a woman..."

Emma's gaze snapped up. "You're dating?"

"No." The word came out quickly. "But I'm..."

A slow smile crept across Emma's face. "Looking?"

Now the color really started to show in Darion's face. "I am. I don't want to come off like a jerk. It's only been six weeks since we broke things off."

"It seems like a lifetime," Emma murmured.

Darion gave a slow nod, then started to smile. Emma smiled back as the old feeling of *bon ami* settled over her, making her heart swell. "We probably would have made it," he said.

"Yes."

"But…"

Emma's gaze locked with his. "Bullet dodged?"

He let out a whoosh of breath. "Totally."

Emma reached across the table then, eased his fingers off the mug and covered his hand with hers. "We're still friends." It was a flat statement of something she needed to be true.

He nodded. "I didn't know if I could do it—go back to being friends. Then I met Esther—"

"Esther?"

"Old-fashioned name. Old-fashioned girl."

Perhaps someone who needed him?

"And things kind of fell into place?" she asked.

"They did. When Selma called, I decided to come back and see if we could hammer out this friendship thing again. I didn't know that she had intentions of marching us back to the altar." Emma squeezed his fingers, then released his hand to pick up her cup and take her first drink. The coffee was no longer hot.

He smiled. "One look at your face and I knew it wasn't the time to hammer things out. If I tried I'd probably be wearing the hammer."

"I was a little hot," she admitted. "But I think that

Selma and I—the whole family, really—are starting down a new path." For a while anyway. Until Selma felt better, and then all bets were off.

"I was glad you were traveling with Jess Hayward. I figured if you needed someone to see you through, he'd be the guy."

"Why's that?" Emma's question came out on a husky note and she cleared her throat.

"You and he had that brother-sister thing going on."

Now Emma blew out a whoosh of breath as she stared down at the table. "Yeah. About that..."

After a few seconds of silence, Darion said, "Not brother and sister?"

Emma gave an adamant shake of her head. "We didn't pursue matters."

Darion frowned at her. "You weren't ready?"

"I was afraid of losing him...like I lost you."

"Loss happens, Em."

She pressed her lips together. "And I've had too much loss in too short of a time."

Darion was unfazed by her flash of annoyance. "Agreed." He fiddled with the handle of the coffee mug. "So where are you now?"

Far away from the guy she wanted to be near. A guy who'd passed through town without so much as a hello. "I guess...I'm hiding out. Again."

"From what?"

"Very good question, that."

"Something you might want to think about."

Emma met his warm hazel gaze. "I don't know that I'll ever be able to come up with an answer."

"Are you happy right now?"

"No."

He gave a slow nod. "Then maybe that's your answer."

She shifted in her seat. "Jess came back to town and didn't come to see me, even though he knew where to find me."

"There could be reasons for that."

"You know Jess. Can you think of one other than the obvious?" Which was that he was done with her.

"Do you want to go through life not knowing?"

Emma clasped her hands together and met Darion's gaze across the table.

That was the million-dollar question.

Chapter Sixteen

You told Selma you wanted to make your own mistakes...

Emma passed a cattle truck and eased back into her lane. Making her own mistakes sounded good in theory. But embarking on a very real journey that could very possibly *be* a mistake felt like another thing entirely. It felt like being posed on top of that cliff that she'd given Selma permission to pull her back from.

Except Selma didn't know where she was or what she was doing. Only Wylie and her father knew. Neither had tried to stop her. In fact, Wylie had offered to care for the Larkin Ranch while she was gone. Emma had taken him up on the offer after clearing it with Skye.

She adjusted her grip on the steering wheel and maneuvered her brother's truck down the freeway exit ramp. A few miles of state highway and she'd be in Cuthbert, the site of Jess's second-to-last rodeo before finals. The site of her showdown.

Had Jess moved on? Written her off?

He hadn't so much as texted her to find out if she'd gotten home okay. That had surprised her at first, and then she'd decided that it was better that way. That didn't keep Jess's silence from hurting—or making her think that in trying to save a friendship, she'd actually lost it. The unfortunate truth was that she hadn't exactly acted like a friend, offering herself up for goodbye sex, then disappearing after he turned her down.

Emma blew out a breath, cringing at the memory. He was right. She would have regretted goodbye sex, because right now she regretted offering. She hadn't left in the most graceful way, and now she needed to straighten things out. Make amends to the guy she'd abandoned on the road.

Try, anyway.

Maybe she'd totally blown things. Maybe he no longer respected her. She should have stayed in little sister mode…except that she couldn't have done that. Being around him made her want him too, too much.

Talk about blowing things.

She pulled into the rodeo grounds and searched for a parking place, finally giving up and pulling into the competitors' area. When she got out of her car, she heard the announcer give a bull-riding score.

The rodeo was almost over and her moment of reckoning was near.

The ticket booth was closed, so Emma walked in without pausing to dig money out of her purse. She eased her way through the people—competitors and rodeo family members—standing at the rail just in time to watch Wes Fremont complete a spectacular ride.

She turned to the cowboy next to her. "Has Jess Hayward ridden yet?"

The old guy shook his head and handed her his battered program.

Man of few words. Emma said thank you and turned back to the rail, quickly checking the lineup. Wes had been the first rider. Jess was second to last. A bull rider she didn't know rode next for all of three seconds. He hit the ground running as the bull threw a hook his way.

"Some tough stock today," the old cowboy murmured without looking at her.

"Mean?"

"From what I've seen."

Emma's stomach tightened as adrenaline kicked in. She'd kept up with Jess. Knew that he was back in peak form. In fact, every ride since she'd left he had been in the money and he was now leading in the standings.

"Em!" She turned to see Dermott come to a stop behind her, his arm in a sling.

"Hey. How're you doing?"

He lifted the arm. "This is what I got for trying to come back too soon."

"Sorry to hear that."

Dermott gave a stoic nod. "We kind of missed you."

"I had some stuff at home to take care of."

The bull being loaded into the chutes started a ruckus, rearing and kicking, and Dermott exhaled loudly. "Chase's bull." He gave Emma a quick smile. "I need to get back there. I'm supposed to pull his rope for him."

Emma smiled her understanding, wondering as he left how he was going to pull the bull rope effectively with an injured right arm.

Focus.

Cliffhanger gave a whistling snort, blowing snot everywhere as Jess placed his boot on the bull's broad soot-colored back, letting the animal know that he was there. He slid down onto the bull close to the flank strap, felt the heat the animal generated through the denim he wore.

His luck had turned since Emma had left. He was winning again, and winning big.

It wasn't enough.

Dermott pulled the bull rope with his good hand and Jess went to work warming the rosin. Once he was ready, Dermott released the tail and he worked his hand into position.

He'd proven to himself that he was ready for the pro circuit. At this time next year, barring injury, he'd be traveling the nation with his brother, chasing the really big money.

That won't be enough either. Not without a sassy-mouthed red-haired girl giving him trouble.

Damn but he missed her. And he didn't know how to fix things. She was living on his sister-in-law's, and good friend's, ranch, but that didn't bring her any closer to him.

He slid forward onto his hand and nodded at the gate man. Cliffhanger reared out and landed on stiff front legs, jarring Jess, tossing him forward. He fought back, pushed deep into his feet.

The bull tossed his head back, missing Jess's face by a fraction of an inch.

Nice try, Cliffy.

Cliffhanger launched off from his hind feet, putting all four in the air as he rolled his shoulder. Jess countered by pushing away the roll, then bracing himself for another stiff-legged landing.

This time it wasn't as jarring because he was ready for it. A mind-bending spin to the right, followed by a reverse spin to the left. Jess started going over his hand but managed to hang on, using the next reversal to regain his center.

The buzzer sounded and Jess pulled his hand free as he swung his boot over Cliffhanger's head and landed on one knee in the dirt.

The crowd was on its feet, but Jess waited until the bull was occupied by the two bullfighters before waving his hat in acknowledgment. The knee he'd landed on didn't feel quite right, but adrenaline kept him going until he got out of the arena.

"Better get to the medic trailer."

Jess nodded at the official who offered the helpful advice and limped on down the alley. As he passed the trailer, he heard his score. Ninety-two. He'd be in the money even if he didn't win, but he was fairly certain the ninety-two would put him on top.

Here he was, living his dream and wishing his life was different.

EMMA DREW IN a shaky breath after Jess had limped out of the arena. Watching him ride had been…amazing. "He did okay."

"Hon, that boy always does okay."

She smiled at the man who'd lent her the program and handed it back to him. "Thank you." He touched his hat and Em turned away from the rail, traveling only a few feet before indecision slowed her steps.

She glanced around and realized that the competitor parking was on the opposite side from spectator parking. She didn't know where to find him. Didn't know who he was riding with or what they drove. And the alley exit that the competitors used was on the opposite side of the arena from where she now stood. Damned backward arena. She needed to get to the opposite side. Fast. She had exactly one day off before she had to be back at the diner for her shift. Skye was depending on her while she was gone.

Emma worked her way around the back of the stands, weaving her way through and around groups of people waiting at the concessions or making their way to the parking lot now that the rodeo was almost over. She squeezed through an opening in a chain-link fence into the competitor parking lot, but it didn't bring her any closer to the alley where she wanted to catch Jess. If she didn't see him leave, or if he had already left…

She dug her phone out of her pocket and started writing a text.

I'm here and—

What?

Of all the times for words to escape her. She knew what she wanted, what she had to do—

"Em?"

She jumped at the sound of the familiar voice and turned as her heart hammered against her ribs, dropping her phone in the process. Behind her was a group of four bull riders—Chase, Dermott, Tim LeClair and Jess. Only one of them was staring at her…the other three were staring at him.

Jess started toward her purposefully, as if zeroing in on a target, his chaps flapping around his legs, the grip bag that carried his rosin, rope and glove in one hand. He bent down, picked up the phone that had skittered several feet away and held it out. Em carefully took it from him without making contact.

She'd planned to say something coherent, such as, "I missed you, so I came to watch you ride," or, "I've done a lot of thinking and I'd like to talk."

Instead she stared at him, trying to read his unreadable expression. And failing.

"I love you."

The words came spilling out, leaving her feeling oddly breathless as the solid truth of what she'd just said slammed into her. She did. She loved him.

Jess's expression didn't change, but behind him the other bull riders exchanged glances.

Em's heart rate was close to redlining, but she pressed on. "I hate being without you." Jess moved closer then, until he was only inches away, dropping his bag in the dirt next to him. She opened her mouth, then closed it again as he solemnly took her face in his hands and tipped her chin up. She swallowed drily. "I know we have a lot to work out—"

"Em?"

"Yes?"

"Stop talking."

"But—"

He kissed her then. Kissed her hard and kissed her long, lifted her off her feet and then set her back down again. There was muttering behind them about getting a room, leaving them be and moving on.

"Great idea," Jess said. "Leave us be."

Tim clapped his back as he went by. "I want to take off in half an hour."

"Yeah. I'll figure out another way to get there. I have business." He looked back at Em, his thumbs brushing over her cheeks.

"Business, you say?" Jess smiled.

"I have missed you so much." His hands slid up into her hair as he kissed her again, making it very clear that he had indeed missed her and was glad that she was there. When the kiss finally ended, he wrapped his arms around her, pulling her close, resting his cheek on top of her head. Held her. The announcer started naming winners, but Jess didn't move. Not even when his own name was called.

Emma eased back. "Congratulations," she murmured.

"Yeah. I won big today."

He wasn't talking about bull riding.

"Me, too," Emma whispered, warmth flooding her body as Jess smiled down at her, looking as if he'd just received the biggest prize of his life.

"Can I ride back to Gavin with you?"

His next rodeo was less than a hundred miles from their hometown. "I'd like that."

He bent down to pick up his bag and looped an arm around her shoulders as they made their way to the parking lot. "I didn't like traveling without you."

"I didn't like it either." She pushed her hair back with her free hand, then took hold of the fingers draped over the edge of her shoulder. "I thought I could slip back into my life after I got home and things would eventually feel kind of normal—that leaving you would be like leaving Darion. It wasn't. You're…part of me, I guess."

His arm tightened and then he let go of her as she slipped back through the gap in the chain-link fence. As soon as he was through, he had his arm around her again. "And you're part of me."

Across the arena, the contractors were loading their animals for the trip to the next event and a steady stream of trucks and trailers moved slowly behind them on their way to the street. Emma barely noticed as the man she loved once again dropped his gear bag, then pulled her close and kissed her again. "You'll never lose me, Em. I promise."

"I seem to recall you giving it a good effort back in the day." She linked her hands behind his back just above the belt of his chaps, loving the feel of his long hard body against hers—right where it should be.

He lightly nipped her lower lip, then gave it a gentle kiss. "Guess I was just waiting for you to grow into that smart mouth."

"And now that I have?"

His arms tightened and he gave her one more quick kiss before whispering against her lips, "I'm never letting you go."

Epilogue

"Now, you're certain that Jess doesn't mind that you're wearing the dress."

Emma somehow managed not to roll her eyes. Selma, who'd been all about wearing *the dress*, was now having second thoughts.

"I think we should get a new dress."

"What do we do with this one?" Emma reached out to touch the soft folds of ultra-expensive silk charmeuse hanging on the back of her closet door.

"Isn't your friend Chloe getting married?"

"She can't afford this dress."

Selma stood back, tapping her finger on her chin. "We'll think of something."

"I'm sure *we* will," Emma murmured. Selma was still a force to be reckoned with, but Emma no longer felt overwhelmed by her stepmom. Maybe because she now had backup, in the form of her brothers, who'd finally realized the benefit of a united front where their mother was concerned, and in Jess, who always had her back.

Damn but she loved that man.

And speaking of Jess… Emma glanced at her phone. "I need to go if we're going to get to Bozeman in time to catch the plane." She could see that the dress thing was going to eat at Selma, so she said, "Why don't you find me something suitable? Surprise me? Something about half the price of this dress."

Selma's expression brightened. "Maybe an off-the-shoulder dress. Something simple, a little pastoral…"

"That would be perfect." Emma reached out and gave Selma a quick hug as the kitchen door open and closed. "I'll call as soon as we get back."

"Em?"

"Coming."

She headed out to the kitchen where her husband-to-be waited with her father and younger brother, who was giving Jess a few last-minute pointers about making it through airport security unscathed. Two trips with Emma to watch Jess ride and suddenly he was an expert.

But the trips had done him good and now he was considering going to college on the other side of the country. Emma thought that would be good for everyone. The rest of the family was still close enough for Selma to manage, and Wylie would develop some much-needed independence.

Jess took her hand, said goodbye to her parents, who wished him luck, then led Emma out of the house. As soon as the door shut behind them, he put an arm around her and dropped a kiss on her head.

"Your dad wants to go in on the construction business. He sees it as a good way to diversify."

Emma gave him a surprised look. Jess had already banked enough money to buy the business outright. He didn't need a partner, but maybe her dad needed to be a partner. To focus on something other than the ranch.

"You sure about this?"

"Totally. We had a long talk. Shared some Len stories. He made me promise to treat you like a queen."

"Sounds like a good talk."

Jess opened the truck door and handed her inside, then settled his hands on her thigh. "Are you all right with the plan?"

Emma gave him a long look, loving the way he took care of her, and his brother, and now her father, before reaching out to press her palm against the side of his face.

"I'm good with anything you want to do," she murmured as she leaned down to kiss him.

"We might have to test that theory."

"We have a plane to catch."

He smiled against her lips. "Then I'm going to have to ask for a rain check."

Emma laughed softly. "You got it, babe. Now let's get out of here so you can go ride a bull."

* * * * *

Be sure to check out
A BULL RIDER TO DEPEND ON—Tyler's story—
as well as the other books in the
MONTANA BULL RIDERS *miniseries,*
THE BULL RIDER MEETS HIS MATCH and
THE BULL RIDER'S HOMECOMING

All available now from
Harlequin Western Romance

#1629 THE TEXAS VALENTINE TWINS
Texas Legacies: The Lockharts
by Cathy Gillen Thacker

Estranged lovers Wyatt Lockhart and Adelaide Smyth have a one-night stand resulting in twin babies. While figuring out how to coparent they discover they are already married!

#1630 HER COWBOY LAWMAN
Cowboys in Uniform • by Pamela Britton

Sheriff Brennan Connelly, champion former bull rider, reluctantly agrees to help Lauren Danners's son learn to ride bulls. But his attraction to the much younger single mom is a distraction he doesn't need!

#1631 THE COWBOY'S VALENTINE BRIDE
Hope, Montana • by Patricia Johns

An IED sent Brody Mason home from Afghanistan, but he's determined to go back. There's nothing for him in Hope, Montana...except maybe Kaitlyn Harpe, the nurse who's helping him to walk again, ride again and maybe even love again.

#1632 A COWBOY IN HER ARMS
by Mary Leo

Callie Grant is stunned—the daughter of her ex and former best friend is in her kindergarten class! Widower Joel Darwood thinks what might be best for him and his child is Callie, if only he can convince her he's changed...

"I never knew you had a bit of a lawyer in you," Amy said.

"No lawyer. I'm just someone who had to raise three scrappy kids while trying to keep a ranch going and earning some sort of a profit. You learn how to put out potential fires before they get started," he told her with a wink.

"You do have a lot of skills," Amy said with unabashed admiration.

Connor had no idea what possessed him to look down into her incredibly tempting upturned face and murmur, "You have no idea."

Nor could he have said what spurred him on to do what he did next.

Because one minute they were just talking, shooting the breeze like two very old friends who knew one another well enough to finish each other's sentences, and then the next minute, somehow those same lips that were responsible for making those flippant quips had found their way to hers.

And just like that, with no warning, he was kissing her.

Kissing Amy the way he had always wanted to from perhaps the very first moment he had laid eyes on her all those years ago.

And the kiss turned out to be better than he'd thought it would be.

Way better.

It wasn't a case of just lips meeting lips, it was soul meeting soul.

Before Connor knew it, his arms had slipped around her, all but literally sweeping her off her feet and pulling her against him.

Into him.

The kiss deepened as he felt his pulse accelerating. He knew he shouldn't be doing this, not yet, not when she was still this vulnerable.

But despite his trying to talk himself out of it, it felt as if everything in his whole life had been leading to this very moment, and it would somehow be against the natural order of things if he didn't at least allow himself to enjoy this for a single, shimmering moment in time.

Don't miss A BABY FOR CHRISTMAS
by Marie Ferrarella, available December 2017
wherever Harlequin® Western Romance books
and ebooks are sold.

www.Harlequin.com

Looking for more satisfying love stories
with community and family at their core?

Check out **Harlequin® Special Edition**
and **Harlequin® Western Romance** books!

New books available every month!

CONNECT WITH US AT:

Harlequin.com/Community

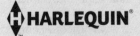

Facebook.com/HarlequinBooks

Twitter.com/HarlequinBooks

Instagram.com/HarlequinBooks

Pinterest.com/HarlequinBooks

ReaderService.com

 HARLEQUIN®

**ROMANCE WHEN
YOU NEED IT**

HFGENRE2017R